For John & Doreen Morgan.

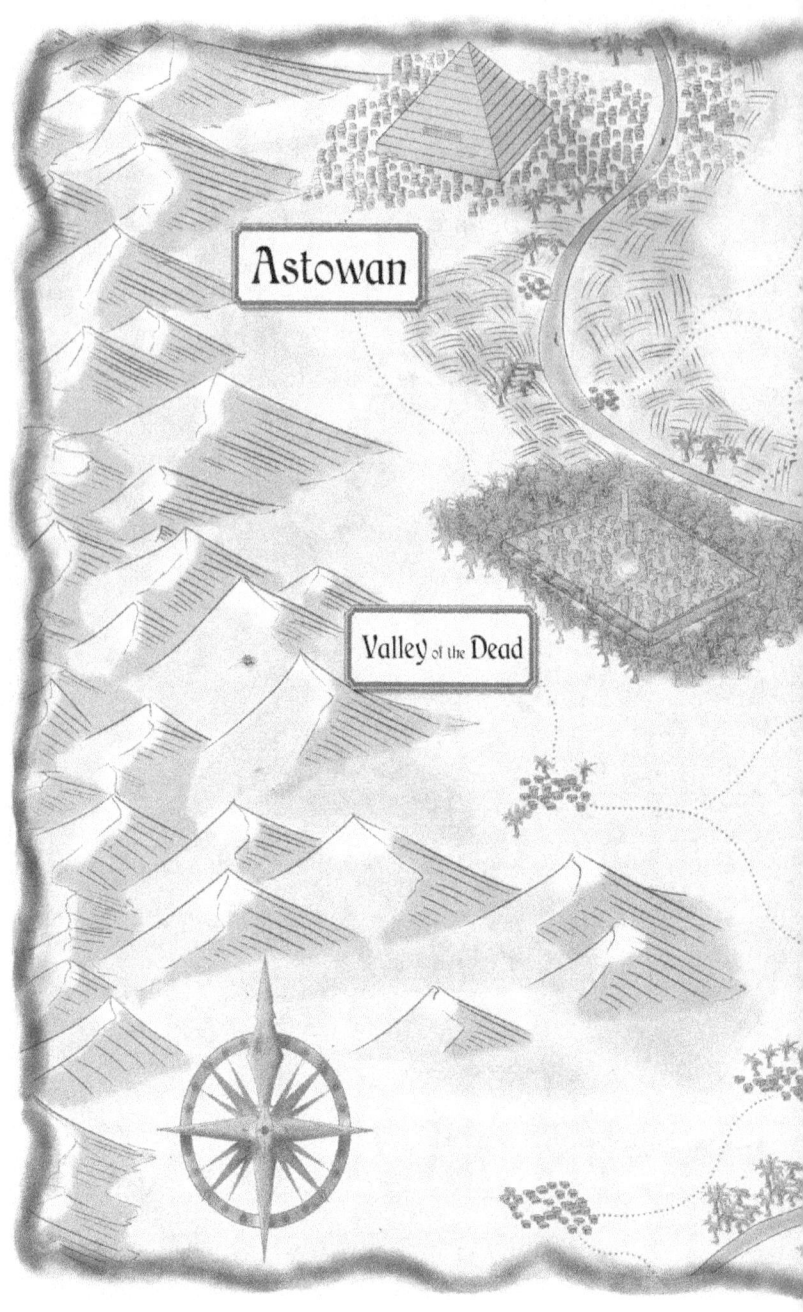

JOSHUA AND THE MAGICAL TEMPLES

PORTALLAS BOOK 3

By Christopher D. Morgan

portallas.com

This novel has been written using British English spelling and conventions.

Joshua and the Magical Temples is book 3 in the *Portallas* series.

Second edition (published December 2017)

Edited by Gordon Long
Cover design by Christian Bentulan

39,231 words.

ISBN-13 (hardback): 978-0-6482145-1-9
ISBN-13 (paperback): 978-0-6482145-0-2
ISBN-13 (e-book): 978-0-9945257-9-6

www.dragonrealmpress.com

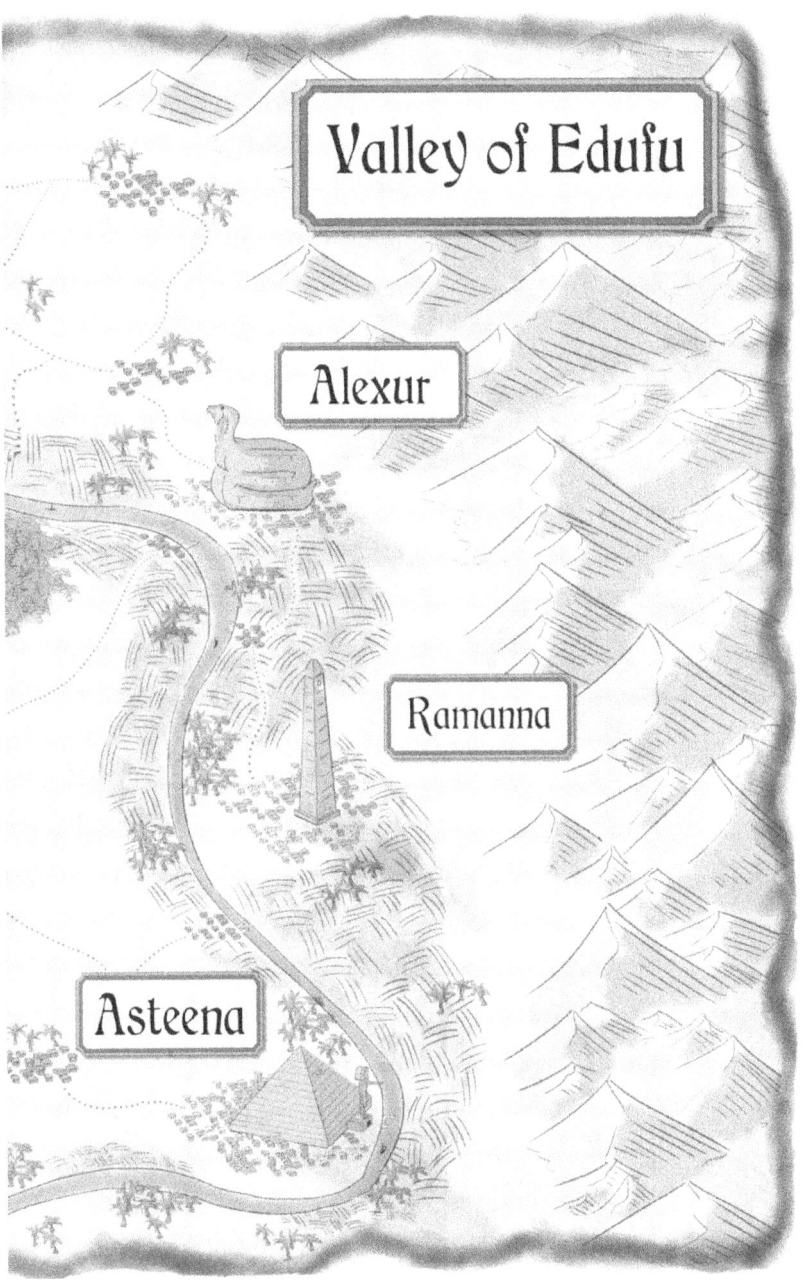

Valley of Edufu

Alexur

Ramanna

Asteena

CHAPTER ONE
King Ahmoses III

"Well? Are they dead?" Queen Neferemu asked. The king didn't respond. He stood there, peering into a small round mirror fixed to the end of a golden staff resting on the marble floor. With both hands gripped around the magical object, he held it to his right eye. King Ahmoses III was either concentrating so hard that he didn't hear his wife or was just plain ignoring her.

"Well?" the queen nagged. "What do you see through the Eye of Horentus? What does it show you?"

"Hush now, my queen! Hard enough it is trying to make out what little the eye will show me without these constant interruptions."

Moments later, the king pushed the staff and mirror away from his eye and let out a sigh. "They are alive, but for how long I cannot say. They have landed in Asteena."

"Asteena?" the queen gasped. "This is at the south end of the valley. For thieves and pickpockets is this place a breeding ground. These children, who will know nothing of this world, nowhere will they be safe in that…that…cesspit. It is a certainty they will not survive long there."

With another sigh, the king slumped onto his golden throne. The magnificent chair had elaborate decorations carved into it and elegant peacock feathers woven into a lattice around its hardwood frame. Intricate gold pressed-leaf patterns twinkled in the light. Plush velvet covered its backrest and seat. The back rose to a point just above the king's head, with a crystal sitting at the apex. Covering the glass ball was a small crown — a symbol of royal status.

The king thought hard, his chin resting on one fist. He tapped the fingers of his other hand on the maroon velvet-clad armrest. His Divine Majesty's eyes shifted as he concentrated.

Displayed around the airy throne room were a dozen guards — six on each side. Each man stood to attention, a spear in his right hand. The leather straps of armour wrapped around their bodies showed their muscular forms. No faces were visible through their warrior's hoods.

Two more guards stood by the door just beyond the twelve steps leading down from the throne. They stood with their eyes fixed on the king through narrow slits in their visors — waiting to obey his next utterance or gesture.

The king reached his hand out to the side, maintaining his glare towards the main door of the chamber. Queen Neferemu took the hand, stroking it.

The king turned to his wife. She was a slender woman with sleek curves, and colourful makeup highlighted her youthful features. Dark lines traced around her enigmatic eyes. A tight, golden, full-length gown clung to her skin, revealing her curvy figure. Sequins glistened in the light streaming through openings high in the stone walls on either side of the room. Her hair was brushed upwards into a cone shape. Golden ribbons crisscrossed the headpiece to tie it all together. She undressed her husband with her eyes.

Without turning his head, the king snapped the fingers of his free hand. A servant hastened forward from the side, carrying a writing block. Upon it were a piece of yellow papyrus and a quill made from a peacock feather, resting next to a stone bowl of black ink.

"Jafar will be their guide," the king declared, taking the quill in his right hand. He wrote on the papyrus. The queen smiled, still caressing.

Joshua and Sarah peered around the cramped space. Bare stone walls hemmed them in on four sides. What little light there was streamed in through gaps in the wooden door. A small candle rested on a stone block in one corner. A hubbub filtered in from outside. The closed door muffled sounds of indistinct shouting and talking. It was confusing. *Why are we here*? *What is this place*?

"These look like bags of wheat or something," Sarah ran her hands over the hessian sacks beneath them. "I think this might be a…storage room, perhaps?"

"Look at these walls," Joshua ran his hand down the smooth yellow sandstone. "I've never seen anything like it. Have you?"

Sarah shook her head. "What do you make of this?"

On the block beside the candle lay a piece of papyrus with a long, colourful feather resting on it. Sarah passed them to Joshua.

"This feather," he said, studying it. "It reminds me of something. But…"

He read the papyrus. He understood the words, but what did it all mean?

> *Hello Joshua. I know this must all be confusing to you. If you can remember her name, then all is not lost. I have left you something to help you. I only pray that some of your memories are intact. If you want to live, you must come at once. He lives, but He is weak. This makes Him desperate and even more dangerous than ever before. You are our only hope, Joshua. I pray your memory is still intact and that you can save us all.*
>
> *- Yours hopefully, His Divine Majesty, King Ahmoses III*

Sarah read with him, then took the feather and studied it. It was a long, blue and red plume but where did it come from?

"What does this all mean?" Joshua asked. "Who is this…King Ahmoses?"

"Luana," Sarah gasped.

Joshua stared at her with a confused expression.

"That's who the girl is," she said with wide eyes. "That's who he's referring to. I'm sure of it. Only…I don't know who she is…or was."

Then the words on the papyrus faded. Within moments, the page was blank. Joshua and Sarah's jaws dropped.

"Look!" Sarah shot her hands to her mouth.

Letters in black ink appeared on the papyrus like an invisible quill was at work—writing before their very eyes. Soon, a new message was complete.

Hello Joshua. You are in Asteena. It is not safe there. You must leave the city immediately and head north. Jafar will find you. You must do as he says. Your lives are in danger so you must act without delay. I hope to see you very soon. Our lives may be in your very hands.

- Yours hopefully, His Divine Majesty, King Ahmoses III

Joshua and Sarah gazed in disbelief at the new message on the papyrus.

"Someone knows you're here," Sarah said.

"But who? Who is this king?" Joshua asked. "Asteena? Where's that? I've never heard of it. Have you?"

He continued to stare at the papyrus.

"How did these words just appear?" Sarah asked. "It's like someone is talking directly to you. And who is Jafar?"

The commotion outside the door drew their attention again. Light pouring through the cracks came and went. People walking by cast moving shadows.

"We only have questions here. Safe or not, I think some of the answers might be out there," Joshua nodded at the door. He rolled up the papyrus and stowed it in his keeper bag.

"There's only one way to find out." Sarah walked over to the door and pushed it open. Joshua followed her out.

Christopher D. Morgan

CHAPTER TWO

Asteena

It was broad daylight outside. Joshua struggled against the brightness until his eyes adjusted. He was standing at the intersection of two bustling streets. There were no trees. In fact, nothing was growing at all. It was unlike anything Joshua had seen before. The buildings on either side of the streets were made from the same yellow sandstone as the room from which they had just emerged.

Dozens of people pushed past each other in both directions. The cacophony of sounds and sights was overwhelming. Wooden carts lined the sides of the buildings, each shielded from the sun by a white sheet strung from a wooden frame attached to the wall. Many carts were piled full of strange fruits and vegetables. Clothing and bolts of cloth draped others. Men sold clay pots, wooden carvings, strange piles of coloured powders and lots of other unrecognisable things.

Stationed at every cart was a trader, pleading with the hordes of passers-by. Each trader attempted to out-shout his neighbours with his sales banter, holding out his fruits or fabrics to tempt the passing shoppers. People shuffling by reached out to feel or smell them. Many brushed the items to the side and kept moving. Some customers were buying things, with coins changing hands. The traders weighed items on primitive hand scales before tipping them into the customers' sacks.

SNAP!

Joshua started, turning towards the noise. A small animal had appeared right out of thin air. The furry creature made a loud snapping sound as it did so. It was brown with short hair all over its body. It had four limbs, each with a hand attached to it, and a long, spindly tail. Tufts of hair ran down the creature's back, and it had huge, pink ears that shifted around. On the front of its round face were large, green eyes.

There were two more snaps, each accompanied by other green-eyed animals appearing. The three beasts climbed onto a cart laden with yellow and green fruits and rummaged through the pile, knocking several to the ground. The first one to appear took a fruit in its mouth and tugged on the outer peel, discarding bits to the ground. As it chewed on the soft inner fruit, the cart's owner, who was tending to a customer, noticed this and grabbed a cane leaning against the wall beside him.

"Hey! Begone, you little…!"

The trader lunged for the animal, slicing through the air with his cane. Before he could reach it, there was another snapping sound, and the critter vanished. The rod landed on top of the fruits where the animal had been sitting, causing more of them to fall to the ground. The trader pulled a scornful face and went after the other two animals. They, too, disappeared with loud snapping sounds before the irate man's cane could connect with them.

"Is nothing safe anymore? This is the fourth Kimalla raid I've had this morning alone," the merchant complained to his neighbour, throwing his hands in the air. "I swear to the kings and gods they are becoming more daring with each passing day. At this rate, I will not have enough to feed even my own starving grandmother before long."

"How we are expected to earn a living is beyond me," the neighbour shook his head in agreement. "Yesterday I lost half my cabbages to these vermin."

The trader with the cane turned and caught Joshua's eye. He froze, looking the two new strangers up and down.

"You are not from here, I think," he said with a knowing smile. "Come, my friend," he said, beckoning them over.

Sarah tugged on Joshua's hand. "Come on," she whispered. "Let's move on."

With another firm tug, Sarah yanked Joshua into motion and led him down the street. He continued looking at the trader until he lost sight of the man, who maintained eye contact until Joshua was out of his line of sight.

The bewildering array of sights and sounds continued their onslaught from every direction. Traders shouted over each other as Sarah led them through the crowd.

"Cabbages, get your cabbages…"

"Come, sir, you will never find a better-quality pair of sandals south of Alexur…"

"A magic potion from the capital city of Astowan! One sip from this vial and you will live for a thousand years, my friend. Come, try and…"

"One juicy bunch of dates. You sir! Just six sickles for the bunch. Four! Okay, three but that's my final—"

They reached the end of the narrow market lane and the last of the trading carts. The throng of people thinned out, providing Joshua with much-needed relief to his senses. The path opened out to a view of a wide river that led away in both directions. Moored along the riverbank were dozens of vessels with white sails furled to booms on heavy wooden masts. Many similar boats were sailing back and forth along the river. Workers along the riverbank were loading and unloading crates from the docked vessels.

"Hey, look at that!" Joshua said, pointing to his left.

There, just down the river, an enormous golden-yellow structure pierced the skyline. Its four triangular sides joined to a point at the top. Smooth on all sloping sides, it rose high into the sky—much taller than any tree Joshua had ever seen. Standing at its base, facing the river, a giant statue of a muscular man—almost as tall as the yellow structure—stood before it. He wore a skirt and a headdress that hung down to his shoulders. His hand was reaching out towards the river.

"I see you are admiring the Pyramid of Asteena, my friend."

The frail, older man standing before them spoke in a high-pitched voice, with a strange accent like those from the market. Like everyone else, he wore a white garment that draped his entire body from his shoulders to his ankles. He smiled at the yellow monument with his arm held out and his palm facing forwards as if proud of the structure he was pointing out.

"It is a most wondrous place and a monument to the king himself. Have you ever seen a majestic sight such as this before?"

"Come on," Sarah said, again tugging at Joshua's hand and peering at the man through narrowed eyes.

"No wait, my friends! Please listen. You are Joshua, are you not?"

"Wait, how do you…"

"I am Jafar," the man cut Joshua off. He bowed, lowering his head almost to waist height and stretching his hands outwards. "From this time forward, I am your faithful servant. Please, come with me. The people of Asteena are not always welcoming to strangers. Come! Follow me, please."

The man walked off towards the river, beckoning over his shoulder for them to follow.

"Jafar!" Joshua exclaimed, turning to Sarah. She still looked suspicious. "Don't you remember? That's the name we saw on the papyrus. It said Jafar would find us."

Joshua followed the small man. This time it was he who tugged at Sarah to move along with him.

Jafar led them along the river and away from the crowds. After several minutes, they approached a rickety old boat that had seen better days. The vessel did not appear fit for the water or even safe to climb aboard. There were no other craft moored anywhere near it. Its white sail was furled to the boom. Ropes tied it to a wooden walkway extending from the bank. The rickety bridge looked like it might collapse under its own weight. The was no sign of anyone aboard.

"Come," Jafar said, leading Joshua and Sarah onto the unstable wooden walkway. "It is safe. This is my felucca. I have something special for you on board."

Sarah continued eyeing the man with suspicion, but she followed Joshua onto the vessel. Once aboard, Jafar led them through a narrow opening in the middle of the deck and down a short set of steps. Below, Joshua looked around, allowing his eyes to adjust to the dim surroundings. Light streamed in from cracks in the upper deck. Deceptively small from the outside, the boat had more space inside than he expected.

It was very untidy below with bits of clothing strewn all around. Bowls of half-eaten food lay piled in various nooks and crannies. Over in one corner, a striped blanket draped over an irregularly shaped object that rose gently up and down. A pair of feet poked from underneath, one crossed over the other.

"Ah, yes," Jafar followed Joshua's gaze to the slumbering figure. "This is the special surprise I mentioned."

He walked over and kicked one foot. "Get up! You have visitors."

The figure jolted and fell to the floor with a thud, then scrambled to its feet, pulling the blanket from its head. There, standing before them, was Joshua's best friend.

"Andrew!" Joshua shouted with surprise.

There was an uncomfortable pause. "Yes?" Andrew looked confused. Instead of beaming with delight, he just stood there with a squint, looking perplexed.

"Andrew?" Joshua asked, tilting his head and lowering his eyebrows.

"Yes? Um…sorry but…who are you, exactly? And…how do you know my name?"

Christopher D. Morgan

CHAPTER THREE
Lost Memories

Joshua and Sarah looked at each other with stunned amazement.

"He has no prior memory," Jafar said.

"What do you mean?" Sarah asked.

Jafar scratched his head and paced back and forth. "Tell me, my friend," he turned to Joshua. "What do you know of your life before you arrived here? Where are you from?"

"Well, I'm from…I'm…um…it's a place called—"

As hard as he tried, Joshua could not remember. Everything was a blank. Sarah and Andrew were familiar, but details of his earlier memories were vague.

"I…I don't understand," he said.

"Hmm," Jafar said. He turned to Sarah. "And you, my dear? What can you tell me of your past? Hmm?"

Sarah frowned, thinking hard. "But this doesn't make sense. I can remember my name and," she turned to Joshua, "I know you are Joshua. But…"

"Your confusion is understandable, my dear."

"How so?"

"Please, sit."

Joshua and Sarah looked around, but there wasn't anywhere they could sit.

Jafar gave Andrew an expectant stare.

"Huh?" Andrew grunted. "Oh, yeah…um. Here, let me tidy up a bit."

He grabbed articles of clothing and blankets lying around to free up two benches. In his enthusiasm, he knocked several bowls onto the floor. Quickly picking them up and composing himself again, he gestured to the now empty seats. Joshua and Sarah both sat.

Jafar leaned against the forward bulkhead and sighed, scratching his head.

"There is a most terrible beast. He has been at war with the king."

"Do you mean King Ah…Ahm—" Joshua tried to pronounce the name from the papyrus back at the market.

"This is the same. His Divine Majesty, King Ahmoses, the third of his name," Jafar bowed, holding his hand to his chest in an intriguing sign of respect. "I am a most unworthy servant, forever in his service. Well, this beast with which the king has been fighting these past years, he has…cast a spell…over the Valley of Edufu."

"The Valley of Edufu?" Sarah asked.

"This is the world in which you now find yourself, my dear. Ah! Where are my manners? On behalf of His Divine Majesty, ruler of this kingdom, I formally welcome you both to the Valley of Edufu."

Once again, Jafar bowed with his hand on his chest, this time directing the gesture to Sarah and Joshua.

"So. Around this world," Jafar continued, "is a magical barrier. It is such that those attempting to pass into this world will have their memories taken from them."

"And that's what happened to us?" Joshua asked.

Jafar nodded. He then gestured to Andrew. "It…affects some people more than others."

"So that's why Andrew can't remember who we are?"

"This is correct. You could very well be Andrew's closest and dearest friend in all the world. He would not know it."

Joshua and Sarah smiled at each other.

"And this…beast you mentioned. Who is that exactly?" Joshua asked, trying to put the pieces of the puzzle together.

"A most wicked and loathsome creature. A half-man and half-beast. He is known to us simply as…the Goat."

Joshua raised his eyebrows at the others. Then, he shrugged and turned to Sarah. "Never heard of him. Have you?"

Sarah also shrugged, shaking her head.

"Hmm," Jafar said. "Something tells me you know more about this beast than you think. The king is hoping this is so. He believes you possess memories—important memories—critical to the king's success in his struggles with this dark creature."

"So how do we get our memories back?" Sarah asked.

"There is a magical orb. We call it the Orb of Memory. This alone has the power to recover what you have lost."

"Where can we find this orb?" Joshua asked.

"Hmm. It just so happens the orb lives right here. It is kept safe inside the Temple of Asteena."

"You mean that big yellow building by the river?" Sarah asked.

"This is the same," Jafar acknowledged with a nod.

"Great. Well, let's go, then." Joshua got up from his bench, clapping his hands together.

"Wait, wait, wait, wait, wait. It is not so easy." Jafar waved his finger at Joshua, who slowly retook his seat. "One cannot simply march into the Temple of Asteena, my friend. The Orb is a sacred artefact, and the people will not take kindly to it being removed. It is a heavily guarded temple. And besides, even if you do make it inside, it will not be easy to remove the orb."

"Hold on. Do you mean to say we have to steal the orb?" Joshua asked.

"Hmm, borrow it, perhaps. This you must do."

"And how are we going to borrow it, then?" Sarah asked. "You said the pyramid was heavily guarded?"

"This is indeed so," Jafar said. "But there is a way to distract the guards—just long enough to get you inside. We will use the Powder of Heka."

"The Powder of what?" Joshua asked.

"Heka," Jafar answered. "It is collected and distilled from rainwater…if you know how. The water that falls from the sky has traces of the magic from the memory-loss barrier. When the guards inhale this powder, it will remove their memory. For a short time, but enough for you to get past."

"And once we're inside?" Sarah asked.

"I will help you find the orb."

"Why are you helping us?" Joshua asked. Andrew sat up at this point and leaned forward.

"It is like I said. King Ahmoses III, long may His Divine Majesty rule, believes you can help him. I am forever his unworthy servant. I will, therefore, help you."

"You said, magic powder?" Andrew spoke up for the first time. He continued to stare at Jafar with a suspicious look on his face.

"This is so," Jafar said. "But we must find it first."

"And where are we going to find this 'magical' powder?" Andrew scoffed. He shook his head as if disbelieving everything he had just heard.

"Hmm. It is not easy to come by, it is true," Jafar said. "The powder is highly illegal. Possession of even the smallest amount will earn you a one-way trip to the bottom of the river. This is by decree of His Divine Majesty himself."

Again, Jafar bowed with his hand against his chest as he uttered the king's title.

"Well, if it's so illegal, where are we going to get some?" Joshua asked.

"Hmm. There are people that can help us for a price, if we know where to look, which I do."

Jafar reached into a cupboard and pulled out a pouch. He handed it to Joshua.

"This should cover the price. We will leave here at sundown. Asteena is a breeding ground for criminals—people who are willing to take risks and not ask too many questions. They are like rats that prefer the cover of darkness. You understand?"

Christopher D. Morgan

CHAPTER FOUR
The Informant

Under cover of nightfall, Jafar led Joshua, Sarah and Andrew off the rickety felucca, and the group made their way into the city. It was no longer the bustling hive of activity it was before; the cobblestone-paved streets lay deserted.

Jafar led them through a maze of dark alleyways. Eyes peered at them from dark corners. Shady figures lingered in doorways. Faint whispers bounced off the stone walls.

After many turns, Jafar stopped at a nondescript wooden door mid-way down a narrow alley. He scanned the street twice. Satisfied nobody was watching, he knocked three times. There was a small rectangular opening in the door about head height. Behind it was a strip of wood, which flicked to one side to reveal a pair of eyes. They looked left and right twice before landing on Jafar.

"Allamakba," Jafar whispered to the owner of the pair of eyes now staring back at him.

The strip of wood shifted back into place again. The latch activated, and the door creaked open. Jafar pushed the door and hastily ushered everyone in, keeping watch over the alley.

Inside, the dark room was dank and musty with a strange haze hanging in the air. A dozen or more locals sat at small tables, chatting to one another. Judging by the hubbub, more people were hidden from view.

Jafar pushed the door closed. There was a metallic sound as the latch engaged. The room went silent. Everyone turned their attention to the four strangers.

"Allamakba," Jafar nodded. People resumed chattering.

Joshua squinted as he took everything in. He had never seen anything like this before. People stared at him through the corners of their eyes. Each time he caught someone glance in his direction, they shifted their eyes back to what was happening on their table. It was unnerving.

The stench in the air was nauseating. Many people had tubes in their mouths, attached to hoses about the width of a finger. These led to a series of glass containers stacked on top of each other. Atop each stack was a bowl with smoke coming from it. The customers were inhaling something through the small pipe and then blowing out white smoke through their mouths and noses. The air was thick with this putrid-smelling fog.

On some smaller tables, two people were rolling pyramid-shaped dice onto a board filled with different coloured pebbles. With each roll, they picked up stones and repositioned them. On other tables, each person held pieces of rectangular card they were each staring at, guarding them.

Jafar walked up to a bar, behind which an obese man was cleaning a glass with a dirty piece of cloth.

"Allamakba," he said to the man. The man said nothing but nodded.

"I am looking for Scarab," Jafar whispered, leaning in and eyeing the man.

The fat man continued to wipe the glass, a scowl on his face. He said nothing, but after a few seconds, he nodded in a particular direction. Jafar followed the man's gaze, then tipped his head at him and walked over to a table on the far side of the room. As the frail man crossed the smoky establishment, vortices formed in the white mist hanging thick in the air.

He arrived at a table where a man sat facing away from everyone. A dim light hung from the ceiling above that table. It showed only the man's outline. On the floor beside him was a small cage. Something was inside — moving.

Joshua squinted but couldn't see much detail through the layers of smoke. Jafar exchanged a few words with the man. Then, he looked at Joshua and the others and beckoned them over with a sharp flick of his head. They made their way across the room. Eyes followed them every step of the way.

They reached the table where the man sat, and the figure extended his hand to one side inviting them to sit. Joshua glanced at Jafar, who nodded. They all sat.

Their contact was middle-aged. It was hard to see at first through the dim lighting. The light above the table hung so low that it didn't illuminate the man's face. Then he leaned into the light. Scars etched the length of his cheek and across his chin. He had a large, lumpy nose. He peered at Joshua through thick, bushy eyebrows.

In the middle of the table was a bowl of brown nuts. The man took one and lowered it to the cage beside him. A small hairy hand reached out and grabbed the treat. The creature chirped a few times, then threw bits of shell to the floor, adding to a pile already there.

"My name is Scarab." The man spoke in a deep rumbling tone, eyeing Joshua up and down. "Jafar here tells me you are looking for some Heka powder."

Two men stared at their table from across the room.

"That's right," Joshua whispered.

"You are new to this place. Let me spare you some trouble, my friend. What you ask is illegal. It would put me at great peril, and I see no reason why I should risk myself for you. My advice to you would be to…go back to wherever it is you came from…and stay there. Asteena is a dangerous place and not somewhere for…" he scanned each of their faces, "…children to be playing."

Joshua narrowed his eyes at the man for a few seconds "Maybe we've come to the wrong place. I'll just have to take my money and go…" He stood up.

The man raised his hand, encouraging Joshua to sit down again.

"It will not be cheap," the man said in a calm tone.

Joshua reached into his keeper bag and tossed the fist-sized velvet pouch onto the table. It landed with a clinking sound next to the small bowl of nuts. Scarab raised one eyebrow. He reached towards it. Instead of grabbing it, he took another nut from the bowl and again passed it down to the creature in the cage by his feet. There was a chirping sound followed by the noise of shells landing on the floor.

Scarab pondered the sack of money for a few moments. He then reached down and opened the front of the cage. Pulling on a rope, he lifted the animal onto the table. It was a green-eyed creature similar to those Joshua had heard the trader in the market call a Kimalla.

The furry animal jumped up and down, chirping, but Scarab maintained a firm grip. Holding the frightened beast by the tail, Scarab then reached into the pouch with his other hand and pulled out a square silver coin. He gave it to the Kimalla, which took it and held it in its mouth.

Scarab untied the rope from the collar around the Kimalla's neck and then released the animal's tail, allowing it to fall to the table. Before it landed, there was a loud snapping sound, and the Kimalla vanished.

Scarab then picked up the pouch with the remaining coins and tucked it under his cloak. He looked at Jafar and said, "Allamakba," tipping his head.

"Allamakba," Jafar replied, returning the gesture. Jafar then motioned at Joshua to follow him. Joshua led his friends to the door, pulled it open and saw them back out into the dark street.

Over on the other side of the tavern, a man wearing a hooded cloak sat in a quiet corner. He removed a small tube from his mouth and exhaled white smoke. It lingered in the surrounding air, like a mist drifting across a lake at dawn.

After the group had left, the hooded man reached down to his feet and raised a small cage onto the table. Hissing sounds were coming from it. The man lifted the latch and carefully lowered the cage door. A scaly two-headed snake slithered out onto the table. Its skin was a shiny black. Red rings encircled each head section and a yellow stripe extended the length of its tail. The snake raised its two heads off the table. The skin over its heads and necks stretched into a hood.

A narrow black tongue extended from each mouth, whipping up and down before being sucked back in again. Both heads of the snake hissed again.

The man leaned forward, staring at the two grotesque heads. "I've found them," he whispered to the snake. "Go now and tell Him; they are in Asteena."

Both snakeheads nodded. They turned, and the snake slithered back into the cage. Moments later, there was a snapping sound. The hissing stopped. The man leaned back in his chair and took another puff from the tube that led to a stack of glass containers by his feet. He exhaled the white smoke, which drifted away into the darkness. A smirk formed on his face.

The Goat paced back and forth in His dark, damp lair. Ribbed horns protruded from either side of His head, curling forwards to form sharp points. An untidy tuft of hair hung from His chin. The Goat grunted, expelling misty puffs of air from his wide nostrils with each breath.

Someone was whimpering on the floor. The Goat walked up to him and struck the poor man with his hoof. The force of the kick was so violent it sent the man rolling. Blood stains trailed a path across the ground to where he came to rest. The Goat strode to the man and stood over him. The man gasped for air, lying in a pool of thick blood, choking. Life ebbed away from him. The man looked up into the silhouette bearing down on him.

"You are lying!" the Goat roared. He shook His head violently.

"I s-swear," the man stuttered. "I know nothing. P-please y-you, m-must believe me."

The Goat glared down at the man on the floor. Blood continued to ooze from multiple wounds on the wretched man's body.

A hissing sound echoed from somewhere out of sight in the distance, growing louder. A second hissing sound joined it. The Goat turned to the noise. Slithering across the floor, a black two-headed snake came into the light. The Goat peered at the snake. Its heads nodded before falling silent.

The Goat growled back down at the quivering mass of flesh and blood still gasping for air by his feet.

"I have found him at last. The boy is in the Valley of Edufu. He will *not* escape me this time."

The Goat raised His head and howled up into the dark vaulted ceiling. The sound reverberated around the dank recesses of the room. A few seconds later, distant hissing sounds rang out. The noises approached from all directions. The sounds grew louder. Two-headed black snakes slithered towards the Goat, one by one coming into the dim light. Their hissing echoed, creating an ear-piercing cacophony of white noise. Soon, there were dozens of them, all slithering around the Goat in a circle.

The Goat raised one hand, and the room fell silent as all the snakes stopped and faced him. The Goat snapped His fingers. "Find him...and kill him." With another flick, they turned and slithered off into the dark recesses again. Soon, they were all out of sight.

The Goat turned His attention back to his captive. His nostrils flared with puffs of smoke blasting from them. The Goat's breathing quickened.

"You…worthless piece of scum! Your services…are no longer required."

With an almighty swipe of his hairy leg, the Goat swung his hoof against the man's head with such ferocity that his entire body spun twice in the pool of blood. When the body came to rest, the man wasn't moving.

CHAPTER FIVE

Magical Powder of Heka

Jafar led Joshua, Sarah and Andrew back to the felucca. He hurried them across the rickety walkway and into the guts of the vessel.

"Jafar, what's going on? What was all that about?" Joshua demanded, once they were back inside and Andrew had closed the door.

"Yeah, Jafar," Andrew scoffed, in a disbelieving tone. "Where's this magical powder stuff you said we were supposed to be getting? I don't see any. Do you?"

"Patience, patience, my friends. It will come. You will see. Now," he clapped his hands together, "we shall eat, yes?"

"Eat?" Andrew blurted. "How do you expect us to eat when…?"

"Actually, I am quite hungry," Sarah said, rubbing her tummy.

"Yes, me too," Joshua said. "Starving. We haven't eaten anything since we arrived."

"But…" Andrew began.

"Patience, my good friend." Jafar put his hands on Andrew's shoulders. "All will become clear. You will see. Sit. Be calm. Please."

Andrew stood there, looking angry. His nostrils flared.

"Sit! Please!" Jafar maintained eye contact with Andrew. Although a small and frail man, there was a quality about him that made it difficult to refuse. Andrew heaved a sigh and took a seat, folding his arms in a huff.

"Now then," Jafar said. "Let me see what we have."

Jafar opened a cupboard, rummaging through a pile of boxes stowed there. He pulled out several yellow and green fruits.

"Here," Jafar passed two fruits to each of them. "You try. Very tasty."

Joshua sniffed the fruit's sweet aroma, then peeled away the pitted skin. Inside was a soft, pale yellow ball. He bit into it, sending juices running down his chin. "Hmmm. That's delicious," he said, wiping his face with his sleeve.

"What do you call these?" Sarah asked, biting into hers.

"It is the fruit of the River Palm. It is good. Yes?"

"Hmmm," she said nodding, taking another bite. "These are very tasty."

Andrew sat with his arms folded.

"Come on, Andrew. Give it a try," Joshua suggested

"Look," Andrew said. "No offence or anything, but for all I know, you and I could be sworn enemies."

"But we're not. We're best friends."

"Yeah? How can you be so sure? You've lost your memory, or had you forgotten?"

Joshua and Sarah looked at each other. They both laughed.

"What's so funny?" Andrew said, pulling an angry face.

At that moment, a Kimalla appeared out of nowhere, right in the middle of the room. Andrew leapt backwards, stumbling to the floor in the process and losing grip of his River Palm fruit, which rolled onto the deck in front of the green-eyed animal. The Kimalla had a square coin in its mouth. In one hand, it held a purple velvet pouch, which it dropped before grabbing Andrew's piece of fruit.

"Oy!" Andrew shouted, reaching for the animal. "Give that back you little —"

Before his hand could reach the Kimalla, the creature disappeared, taking Andrew's fruit with it.

Jafar bent down and picked up the velvet pouch. He undid the string, reached inside and pulled out a glass vial, which he held up to the light and shook.

"Aha!" he said. "Did I not tell you to be patient? This, my friends, is Powder of Heka." Jafar raised his eyebrows at Andrew.

37

"Okay," Andrew mumbled in resignation. "Give me another one of those fruits, then."

"So, does this mean we can go to the temple and get the orb?" Joshua asked.

"It does."

"Great! When do we go?"

"We cannot go now."

"What do you mean?" Andrew asked. "You said we needed to go to the temple once we had this magical…whatever it was you called it."

"Power of Heka. This is true. But we do not go tonight. We go in the morning—before the sun is rising."

"Why is that, Jafar?" Sarah asked.

"The Orb of Memory; it is a magical thing. But for it to work, it must remain on the altar. At the time of the rising of the sun, the light will pass through the eyes of the statue and then through the orb and into your eyes. Only then will the memories that have been taken from you be returned. It will not work any other way."

"So, we have to be inside the pyramid and standing in the right place and at the right time for all of this to work?" Andrew asked.

"This is so," Jafar said.

"And then we'll get our memories back?" Joshua asked.

"This I hope."

"This you *hope*?" Andrew said with raised eyebrows, his scepticism once again showing through.

"We will see. Your memories will return, or they will not. We will see. It may be that some of your memories will return, but others will not."

"And what if that happens?" Sarah asked. "Can we just do the same thing the next day?"

"This is so. But…" Jafar paused.

"But…what?" Asked Andrew, shaking his head.

"At the south end of the River of Edufu is the city of Asteena. This is where you are. Asteena is but one of five great temples you will find on the great river that runs through the Valley of Edufu. If your memories are not returned to you here, you must travel north to the next temple, and again use the Orb of Memory. Until your memories are returned, you must visit each temple in the valley. Only once will the Orb of Memory work in each temple. If you reach the capital city of Astowan at the north end of the Valley of Edufu and your memories are not returned…"

There was a long pause. Jafar wore a concerned look on his face.

"What? What will happen if our memories aren't recovered by then?" Joshua asked, leaning forward.

"Well," Jafar said, with a nervous chuckle. "Let us hope it is not so."

An awkward silence descended as everyone's eyes shifted to each other.

Jafar clapped his hands together, breaking the tension. "So. Now we rest. Yes? We must leave early. Come. Sleep."

Christopher D. Morgan

CHAPTER SIX

The Temple of Asteena

"Joshua…"

Joshua's senses stirred. The sound of his name echoed in his mind. Something moved his body. Was it real? He wanted to ignore it—drift away again.

"Joshua!"

The awareness of Joshua's surroundings inched closer to reality. Images formed and disappeared again. Thoughts twisted and turned. Hazy and indistinct memories meandered through his head. Each fleeting image soon faded, replaced by another.

They didn't last long—just enough to trigger the next memory. Were they real? Was he dreaming?

"JOSHUA! WAKE UP!"

Joshua woke to a sharp jolt. The outline of a figure stood over him in the dark. Who was it? Someone poked at his shoulder.

"Joshua, wake up. We go now. Yes?"

Joshua rubbed his eyes. The realisation hit him, and he remembered where he was. He pushed himself up into a seated position to find Sarah and Andrew sitting on the benches eating. Andrew was surrounded by a mess of fruit peel and nut shells.

"Andrew, are you incapable of keeping things tidy?" Sarah complained.

Joshua couldn't quite see what they were chewing on, but Sarah handed him some. Stretching his arms, he yawned.

"What time is it?" Joshua asked, taking a bite out of whatever Sarah passed him.

"It is one hour before sunrise. It is time. We must go."

Once they had all eaten, Jafar led them off the boat. They tiptoed across the rickety walkway, which creaked under their weight. Part way along, one plank Joshua stepped on gave way with a loud crack. He sank halfway through the hole, his foot dipping into the water below. Sarah grabbed him in time and pulled him to safety. Ripples of water appeared from several directions. They converged on the spot where Joshua's foot entered the water.

"Be careful," Jafar whispered. "The River Slicers below are hungry, too."

Jafar led them along the creaking walkway and towards the pyramid.

The deserted streets were eerily quiet. It was a bright night with no clouds, and a half-moon provided just enough light to see where they were walking. A haze drifted over the calm river. The vessels on the water were all moored at the riverbank. Nothing moved along the waterway. Now and then, ripples spread across the water's surface.

The temple-pyramid towered over the city blacking out half the stars from the sky. The outline of the massive statue of the king cast an equally vast silhouette. It grew endlessly bigger as they approached.

There was a square hole in the side of the pyramid facing the river. It was towards the top, at about the same height as the statue's head.

Two men stood to attention on opposite sides of an opening at the statue's feet, each with a spear in his right hand. They wore leather straps around their arms, shoulders and waist and each had a hood with a narrow strip to see through.

"Halt! Who goes there at this hour?" Both guards held their spears pointing at the approaching group.

"A glorious morning, my friend," Jafar said. He reached into his cloak and pulled out the velvet pouch.

"I said HALT!" The guard shouted. "Who approaches the Temple of Asteena?"

"A thousand apologies, my friends. Do not be alarmed. It is me. Do you not remember?"

The guards looked at each other.

"Here," Jafar held the vial of powder up to the guard's face. "ACHOO!"

Jafar blew across the top of the vial. Fine grains of glistening powder flew out and into the faces of the guards. They stepped back, wafting their hands in front of them.

Moments later, the guards turned to each other.

"Um…"

"It is fine, my friend. You are here to protect us. You remember now? Yes? It is a vital job you have. You are to stand here and make sure we are not disturbed. Yes?"

Once again, the guards looked at each other. They shrugged.

"Um…fine. Yes, sir. We won't let anyone in. You can count on us."

With a beaming smile, Jafar stood aside and gestured for Joshua and the others to enter.

He then turned to the guards. "That's it. Well done. I will be sure the king knows how well you have performed your duties."

"Thank you, sir, a thousand blessings to you." Both guards stood again to attention with their spears in their hands and their chests pushed forwards.

Joshua entered the narrow passage followed by Jafar and the others. A minute later, he walked into a great hall. Burning torches along the walls of the chamber illuminated the open expanse. The ceiling stretched up to a dizzying height. High in the air at the back wall of the enormous room was a ledge with an opening behind it.

"It is the altar," Jafar whispered, following Joshua's gaze. "That is where the Orb of Memory resides. That is where we must go. Come. The guard's memories will return to them before long. We must not be here when that happens."

The small man led them to an opening in the left wall. He took a flaming torch from beside the entrance and beckoned them through. The narrow passage was low enough that even Sarah had to duck. The flame charred the ceiling.

They followed Jafar through a labyrinth of corridors. He stopped at an intersection, scratching his head.

"Which way is it?" Joshua whispered.

"I am not sure," Jafar said, concentrating hard.

"What do you mean, you're not sure?" Andrew chided. His irritated voice echoed through the tunnels.

"Shh! A long time it has been. This way, I think."

He turned right, and they continued. Soon they reached a stone staircase and made their way up. It went well beyond the torch's ability to light the path ahead. At the top, they made several more turns.

"Aha. It is here," Jafar said, huffing and puffing. He gestured to Joshua, inviting him to enter.

Christopher D. Morgan

CHAPTER SEVEN
The Orb of Memory

They all followed Joshua into the small chamber. There, atop a stone altar about waist height, was a gold pyramid. Its four triangular surfaces glistened in the pale light. Resting on the top of the pyramid was a spherical crystal. Joshua walked up to the altar and stared at the orb. Carved into one side was a human head outline. In front of the stone plinth was a ledge with an opening above it, like a vast window. It was a long way down.

Below him was the enormous expanse of the great hall. At the bottom was the tunnel where they had entered. In front of him, at about the same elevation as the altar chamber, a square hole led to a narrow shaft. Through it, the statue's outline was just visible. The day was dawning with first light beyond the river in the distance.

"Hey, look at that!" Andrew pointed to the top of the wall above the altar.

Dawn shone through the eyes of the statue, along the shaft and across the great hall. Two pale balls of light struck the back wall of the altar chamber. As the sun rose, they crept down towards the orb.

"The sun. It is rising," Jafar said. "Soon it will be time. You must be ready. Come quickly! Stand behind the altar."

Joshua, Sarah and Andrew positioned themselves between the altar and the back wall, facing the small pyramid. They stared at the orb, beyond which was the ledge leading to the great hall and the front of the temple. The rays of light brightened as they streamed through the square hole and across the expansive chamber.

The balls of light on the wall behind them became much brighter as the sun appeared on the horizon. They were like eyes making their way closer and closer to the orb.

Joshua stared at the crystal, reaching for Sarah's hand. She reached out and clasped his hand in hers. The balls of light were seconds from the orb.

"STOP!"

A guard stood at the entrance to the chamber. His spear was pointing right at them.

Jafar reached his hand out to the guard. "Ah, my friend—"

The guard shoved the frail old man to the side, sending him tumbling. The balls of light were now a brilliant white and moments from reaching the orb.

"STEP AWAY! NOW!" He approached the altar with his spear poised to launch at them.

Jafar threw the vial of Heka to Joshua. Joshua unstoppered it and blew across the open top towards the guard, releasing a cloud of powder into the air. The air around the guard glistened, and he stood there, dazed. His spear clattered the ground.

Then, there was a blinding flash as the intense ray of sunlight struck the orb. The crystal glowed with a blue halo. Brilliant rays of light emanated from it in all directions. The altar chamber lit up as if the sun was right there with them.

Moments later, the chamber darkened again.

"Quickly! RUN!" Jafar shouted.

Joshua grabbed the orb. Sarah and Andrew helped Jafar to his feet. The guard looked around, scratching his head.

They ran past the confused man and out of the chamber. The last to leave, Andrew stopped and said to the guard, "You stay here and, um, carry on guarding!"

"Right, sir. As you wish, sir."

Andrew sped off down the corridor, shouting over his shoulder, "Good work. Carry on."

"Yes, sir. Thank you very much, sir. A thousand blessings to you."

Leaving the guard standing at attention, Andrew caught up with the others.

They flew down the stone stairs and through the maze of tunnels into the great hall. It was now much brighter.

They were halfway across the marble floor when Jafar stumbled. Joshua and the others stopped and ran back to help him. As they did, guards came running into the great hall from tunnels at the rear.

"Joshua!" Jafar shouted. "Take the felucca and head north for a day. You must find the Temple of Ramanna."

"We can't just leave you here."

Guards closed in on them.

"I will be fine. Go! QUICKLY!"

Joshua, Sarah and Andrew left Jafar and continued running towards the main entrance. Once there, they sprinted through the narrow tunnel. Footsteps chased after them. The trio reached the end, emerging into the dawn light. The two guards were still there.

"Oy! Who are you? You're not supposed to be —"

"The powder, Joshua!" Sarah shouted. "It must have worn off."

Joshua reached for the vial of Heka powder. There was a little left inside. He blew it into the faces of the guards.

"Right. Several people are trying to escape," he said, struggling to catch his breath. "Your job is to stop them from coming out of this tunnel, understand?"

The soldiers hesitated before nodding.

"You can count on us, sir." They then ran into the tunnel.

Joshua, Sarah and Andrew sprinted back along the riverbank towards Jafar's felucca. Clanging sounds came from the tunnel as they sped away. A line of guards emerged from the temple entrance, searching for the fleeing outsiders.

"RUN!" Joshua screamed.

They reached the boat and ran across the rickety walkway, huffing and puffing. Several planks creaked as they raced onto the felucca. Andrew, the last aboard, tripped as one of the wood struts gave way beneath him. He stumbled onto the vessel as pieces of wood fell into the river.

"Right," Joshua cried. "How do we get this thing moving?"

Andrew shrugged.

"The sail," Sarah said. "We need to lower the sail."

Half a dozen guards approached their position on the riverbank. The rigging was a tangled mess. One line coming from the mainsail led to an anchor point on the side rail.

"That one there! Hurry! You're the best at knots," he shouted at Andrew, pointing to where the rope was tied off. Andrew ran to untie it, while Joshua and Sarah fumbled with the mooring lines.

The first three guards reached the wooden bridge with three more close behind. They shoved at each other, each trying to be first onto the boat.

"Quickly Andrew!" Joshua screamed.

Andrew untied the rope as fast as he could. The three jostling guards finally made it onto the walkway. The three behind them followed, scampering along the creaking framework when —

CRACK!

The wooden structure gave way under the weight of the heavy soldiers.

SPLASH!

The whole thing, along with all six guards landed in the river. As the men thrashed their arms trying to find a footing in the deep water, ripples formed from all around the vessel.

"ARGHHH!"

One guard submerged. Another followed, then another. More ripples sped towards them from other directions. There was more splashing, and then silence. A few bubbles broke the surface, but then the ripples faded, leaving the waters calm again.

Andrew released the rope, and the sail dropped from the horizontal boom hanging across the main mast. The white sail caught the wind, and the felucca drifted away from the riverbank. He ran to the back of the boat and grabbed the rudder, pushing it left and right to steer the craft.

Soon, they were out into the middle of the river and sailing north. There was no activity behind them. As they sailed away from the city of Asteena, the outline of the pyramid and statue glimmered in the dawn light.

Joshua looked back. *I wonder what happened to Jafar.*

CHAPTER EIGHT
A memory returned

Andrew steered the felucca north up the river. With the sun now rising high into the sky, the city of Asteena with its majestic golden pyramid and regal statue faded from view. It wasn't until an hour had passed with no activity behind them that Joshua was convinced nobody was following and he could at last start to relax. A gentle breeze blew against his face as the boat drifted across the calm waters.

The riverbank was twenty or more boat lengths away on either side. Swathes of green, brown and yellow fields stretched beyond the edges of the river. In some tracts, farmers tended their crops. Beyond this patchwork of colour were rolling foothills with white-peaked mountains in the distance. North and south, the valley stretched to the horizon.

Clusters of reeds dotted the riverbanks. Now and then a disturbance in the water created concentric circles of ripples expanding outwards. What creatures lurked beneath the surface, powerful enough to drag grown men to their deaths?

Joshua closed his eyes and tried to put it all out of his mind. He took a deep breath and exhaled, puffing his cheeks. The young man wanted to collect his thoughts. For the first time in as long as he could remember, he wasn't in a state of heightened anxiety. He didn't know why this was. He was glad for a moment to reflect. Something told him it wouldn't last, so he tried to make the best of it while he could.

With his eyes still closed, he was enjoying the gentle breeze on his face when a hand rested gently on his shoulder. He smiled.

"Can you remember anything more now?" Sarah asked.

Joshua opened his eyes and took in another fresh lungful of air. He turned to Sarah. "I know I love you. Even more than I did before."

Sarah smiled at him. She brushed the hair out of his eyes, caressing his cheek with the back of her hand. "I love you too, Joshua. It's the one thing I am sure of."

"Okay, okay, you two," Andrew said, approaching from the rear. "Let's all agree that we all love each other."

"What about you?" Joshua asked his friend.

"Yes, yes, yes, I love you, too."

"No, I mean have any of your memories returned?"

"Oh, well," he said with a sigh. "I remember enough to know I should apologise for my behaviour yesterday. It seems we are best friends. Memory or not, I think you proved that through your actions back there."

"Consider yourself forgiven," Joshua chuckled. "I know where I'm from now."

"Morelle," Andrew said. "Yeah, I'm from somewhere called Temerelle, although I think we grew up together. Not quite sure how that works, though."

"What about you?" Joshua asked Sarah. "You're from—"

"Jemarrah," they all said together.

"But those places—Morelle, Temerelle and Jemarrah—they aren't in this world," Sarah said. "We're all from a world called Forestium."

"But we haven't been there for a while now," Andrew said. "I mean, it feels like we've been away from home for some time. At least it does to me."

"Me too. But where *have* we been?" Joshua asked them both. "We've been here in…what's this place called again?" he asked Sarah.

"Oh, um…the Valley of Edufu, Jafar called it."

"Right, we've been here in the Valley of Edufu for a day or so. If we haven't been in Forestium for a while, where else have we been?"

Andrew and Sarah shrugged at each other.

"Maybe some of the answers are waiting for us up ahead," Sarah said with a heavy sigh.

"Well, at least we have some idea of what we need to do to get our memories back," Andrew said.

Joshua nodded. He reached into his keeper bag and pulled out the Orb of Memory. He held it up to the light, and they all studied it.

"There's something…I don't know…something's familiar about this orb." Sarah said.

Andrew nodded.

"Yeah," Joshua said. "I have a similar feeling. I mean, I've never seen this thing before, yet, it's like…somehow, I have. I can't explain it."

"It could be from one of your forgotten memories?" Sarah suggested.

"Perhaps," Joshua shrugged. There was something else. He looked up and stared into space for a few moments, concentrating hard. "Galleon."

"Yes! Galleon!" Sarah gasped. "What happened to Galleon?"

"He was with us before," Andrew strained to recall.

Then there was silence as all three of them struggled to remember any further details.

"Well," Sarah clapped her hands together after a long pause. "At least some of our memories have returned. Hopefully, that means more will do so when we get to Ramanna. I just hope that's where this river takes us. In the meantime, I think we should look around and take stock of what's on the boat. Jafar said it'll take us a day to get there. I hope he has enough for us to eat and drink."

"That's a good point," Joshua said, putting the orb back into his keeper bag. "Let's go below and check."

"I'll have to keep hold of this rudder," Andrew said, "because if I let go for too long, the dratted boat heads towards the riverbank."

Joshua and Sarah climbed through the opening on the main deck and down the small flight of stairs while Andrew stayed in the stern of the boat.

After their eyes adjusted, Joshua and Sarah rummaged around. They searched various cupboards and other nooks and crannies. Two crates contained a variety of different fruits. Sarah located a container of fresh water tucked inside a cupboard.

"Looks like there's more than enough here to keep us going," Sarah said after they had finished taking stock of everything.

"What do you think we'll find in Ramanna?" Joshua asked, slumping onto a bench.

Sarah shook her head and pursed her lips. "Jafar said there were five temples along the valley. I'm assuming one is there."

"Hmm. Let's hope so. Otherwise, we're stuck."

Then, Joshua's eyes lit up. "Hey! Wait a minute," he said springing to his feet. He opened his keeper bag and pulled out the rolled-up piece of papyrus they had found yesterday. "Maybe there's a new message or something that can help us."

"It's worth a try. Well, open it up then," Sarah urged.

Joshua unrolled the papyrus. To his annoyance, it was blank. His shoulders sank, and he let out a deep sigh. He rolled it up again, stowed it back into his keeper bag and slumped back onto the bench.

Christopher D. Morgan

CHAPTER NINE

The Queen's Frustration

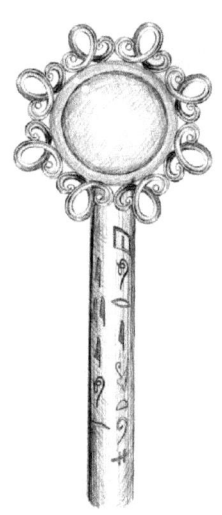

Queen Neferemu lay on her front with her slender feet raised into the air and crossed. Her curvy figure melted into the soft surface of the royal bed. She wore a beautiful purple nightgown made of silk. It ran the full length of her body, clinging to every curve. The gown shimmered in the light, contrasting against the white bedclothes.

She caressed the king's head, tracing her finger up and down his temple. He was lying on his back at a right angle to his wife. Their colossal mattress sprawled in all directions. White sheets as big as felucca sails spread out across the enormous bed. A dozen ornately decorated square velvet pillows filled with the softest feathers were stacked against the golden headboard. The queen stretched out her arm to one side. Her tight-fitting gown slid effortlessly over the satin linen.

The king looked up into the purple, gold-encrusted plush fabric draped over the four-poster bed. The king's bed was in the centre of the huge royal bedroom, raised on a stone plinth. Finely decorated vases and other beautiful objects stood on stone pillars on either side of the windows. Drapes made from the same fabric adorning the bed hung pleated on either side of each window.

"I am trying to concentrate," the king said in an annoyed tone. He wafted the queen's hand away from his forehead.

"Fine," the queen said, rolling over onto her back and stretching both arms out. "But you will learn nothing lying here, doing nothing." She spoke in a sensual tone.

The queen sat up and shifted over to the row of pillows. She lay against them, pushing her chest out and rubbing her hand seductively down the side of her body.

"Come, my darling," she said in a deep, coy voice. "I will give you something to concentrate on." She flicked her head backwards and slid down the pillows onto her back again with her arms stretched outwards.

The king sat bolt upright, turned to the queen. "You are right, my queen. I will not learn anything here. I will again look through the Eye of Horentus."

He leapt from the bed and walked over to the corner where the wooden staff with the mirror stood.

The queen huffed. "What is it that is so interesting about this youngster, my love?" She whined like a moody child. "What is it he does that commands your attention?"

The king didn't reply. He pulled the mirror close to his face and squinted into it with one eye closed.

The queen huffed again. She tapped the satin sheet with her finger, turning her head to one side as if disinterested in what the king was doing.

"It is not what he does, my love," the king said in a slow, contemplative tone, all the while continuing to squint through the small mirror. "It is what he has in his head that interests me."

The queen let out a big sigh. She looked around the room as if bored.

The king pushed the staff forward and opened his eyes again.

"Well…?" the queen feigned interest.

"It is hard to see, my love. I do not think he is in Asteena anymore."

"Oh, really, my love," the queen didn't even bother to look in his direction.

"He is on a felucca. With any luck, Jafar will have already begun to restore the boy's memories. Let us hope it is so."

"Let us hope it is so indeed, my love," the queen drawled. She then threw herself onto her back and let out another deep sigh.

Leaning the staff back in its corner, the king sauntered around the bed with his hands behind his back.

"*If* Jafar has followed my instructions precisely," he pondered, thinking hard. He put one foot carefully in front of the other, staring at the floor as he went, "then the boy *should* be on his way to Ramanna. This is why he is on a felucca. Do you not agree?"

"What do I think?" the queen said, spurred on by the sliver of attention the king tossed her way. She flicked her head again, this time licking her lips and saying in a seductive tone, "I think you should come back to bed, my darling."

The king walked over to the bed and sat on the edge. His wife's eyes lit up with a burst of interest. She crawled on all fours across the bed, put her hands on the king's shoulders. "Tell me, my darling, what can I...do for you?"

The king turned to her, raised his hand towards her face, then snapped his fingers. Within seconds, a servant appeared bearing his writing block, along with the bowl of black ink, a peacock feather quill and the blank piece of yellow papyrus. The king took the beautiful quill and wrote. The queen watched over his shoulder, all the while caressing him.

CHAPTER TEN

A River Encounter

By the time the sun was overhead, Joshua, Andrew and Sarah
had eaten. They were out on the deck, watching the patchwork
of fields drift by. With the morning's excitement now well behind

them, they found time to unwind. The wind had carried them slowly but persistently north through the valley. For hours, they had not seen another vessel. In fact, other than the odd farmer in a distant field, they had seen no activity or signs of life.

"I wonder how far up the river Ramanna is," Andrew pondered out loud.

Joshua shook his head, staring hypnotically into the distance. "Jafar didn't say."

Sarah sat up and leaned forward, squinting. "What's that?"

Joshua stood up and walked to the front of the boat. Farther up the river, something was coming around a bend. "It looks like…it's another boat," he called back to them.

Andrew and Sarah joined him. Peering through the glare of the sun, they held their hands to their heads to create shade. As the vessel approached, there was movement on board. A man was walking around the deck, adjusting the sail rigging.

"What do you think?" Sarah asked Joshua.

"Well, it looks like there's just the one person on board."

"That we can see, at least."

"Hmm. Hold on. I think he's seen us. He's…raising the sail. I think he means to stop."

"We should stop," Andrew said.

Joshua and Sarah both looked at him.

"Well," he said, "maybe he can tell us how far it is to Ramanna. He is coming from that direction."

"He's right," Joshua nodded to Sarah. "Besides, we don't want to arouse any suspicion."

Andrew walked to the side of the deck and pulled on a series of ropes. Bit by bit, he raised the mainsail until the whole thing scrunched up tight against the boom. The boat slowed.

As the approaching vessel drifted up to them, the man there threw a rope to Andrew, who tied it off, securing the boats together.

"Good day to you, captain," the man called over to Joshua. "The grace of the king be with you." As he said this, he held his hand to his chest and bowed.

Andrew extended him a hand, and he climbed on board.

"I am Captain Akhbar, your humble servant," the man jumped onto the deck. "And who do I have the pleasure of speaking with?"

"Hi. I'm Joshua. This is Andrew and Sarah."

Captain Akhbar tipped his head at Andrew. He turned to Sarah with a beaming smile. "My word, what a precious jewel. My tedious journey has been brightened by the grace of your beauty, young lady." He lowered his head and kissed Sarah gently on the back of her hand, causing her to blush.

The man turned to Joshua and asked, "May I ask what is your cargo and where you are heading, Captain Joshua?"

"Oh, well, we're not carrying cargo. We're just trying to make our way to Ramanna."

"Ramanna? I see," Captain Akhbar said, nodding. "It happens I have just come from Ramanna myself. I am carrying wheat from The Valley of the Dead to Asteena. A couple of days I spent in Ramanna. I have a cousin there."

"How far is Ramanna from here?" Andrew asked.

"Not far. By nightfall you will arrive I think, by the grace of the king. What business have you in Ramanna?"

"Oh, um, we're…" He paused with his mouth open, wanting to speak but unable to find the words.

The man squinted at Joshua, and his smile faded.

"W-we're going to visit the temple there," Sarah jumped in to break the awkward silence.

"Ah," the captain exclaimed, his smile forming again. "The temple, of course. Many people from all over come to Ramanna for this. The obelisk is indeed a most wondrous thing to behold. It is even said a magical power lies somewhere buried deep within the temple."

"Magical power?" Joshua asked, with raised eyebrows.

"If you believe," the captain chuckled. "Of course, such things are simply tales and superstitions. But the people come all the same, and they listen to the stories of the charlatans who prey on the tourists." He shook his head. "Farmers and people with little education—they are easy prey for those who will take such advantage."

"Well, this is our first time visiting Ramanna," Joshua said. "We'll watch out for those charlatans. What else can you tell us about the city?"

"Not much is there to tell," he replied, tilting his head and shrugging. "You will do well to avoid the Wadjets when you are there. Horrible beasts."

"What did you call them?" Andrew asked.

"Wadjets. A two-headed snake. Very quick—very venomous. The bite from even one head can kill a man in minutes. It makes a hissing sound. If you hear the sound, it may already be too late."

"This obelisk," Sarah said. "What does it look like?"

The man retook Sarah's hand with a smile. "Like a beautiful beacon, it is pointing to the heavens. From a distance, you will see it. But by the grace of the king, I swear it has a beauty that does not shine as much as yours, my dear." Once again, he bent forward to kiss Sarah on her hand. Once again, Sarah turned a deep shade of red.

Andrew caught Sarah's eye and struggled to hold back a smile.

"Well, my friends," Captain Akhbar said, standing up straight again. "The recipients of my cargo await. It has been a long journey, and I have not had the favour of the wind. My food supplies are low."

"Oh, well, we have plenty. You're welcome to some," Joshua said.

The captain tipped his head. Andrew went down to the lower deck and came back toting a crate full of River Palms with an assortment of nuts and some leafy green vegetables stacked upon it.

"You are indeed most kind, my friends. I am forever in your debt," he said, accepting the crate from Andrew with a nod. "May the grace of the king be with you."

As he was climbing off the boat, he turned and said, "Ah, there is something more I forgot to mention. A curious thing that I saw in Ramanna. A strange, half-man you will find there if you visit anywhere near the temple. A curiosity, if you will. They say he was sent to them by the gods. It is said that good fortune awaits he who touches the head of this half-man." He chuckled as he turned and continued climbing off the boat "Well, if you believe in such things, of course. Charlatans! There is nothing they will not do to take advantage of the poor." He waved goodbye, calling out, "May the grace of the king be with you."

Joshua helped the captain release the ropes that tethered the two vessels together. Andrew then released the lines that held their own sail in place. It unfurled and caught the wind. Their boat sailed away, resuming its journey north along the valley.

They waved at Captain Akhbar as they continued.

Christopher D. Morgan

CHAPTER ELEVEN

Arriving in Ramanna

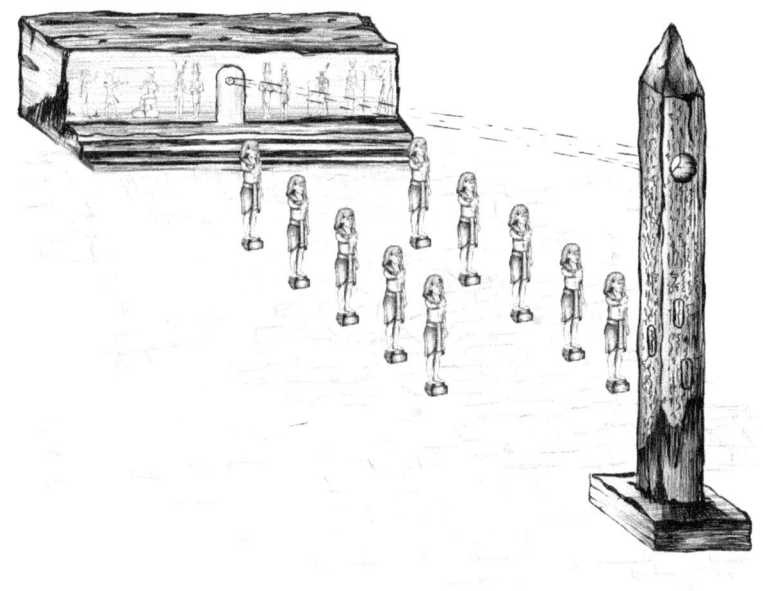

Later that afternoon, more vessels passed them on the river. There were more farmers tending fields, and the riverbanks bustled with activity. A shimmering pointed structure came into view ahead of them.

As they neared the city of Ramanna, Andrew had to work hard to avoid colliding with dozens of feluccas all coming and going. He navigated a path through to an empty slot along the bank. With the boat moored, Joshua, Andrew and Sarah stepped off and wandered into the city. Before he left, Andrew stuffed his pockets with River Palm fruits.

Ramanna was a bustling place, filled with square buildings made from the same yellow sandstone they had encountered in Asteena, although more densely packed and taller. Small crowds gathered at intersections. Individuals stood on stone plinths, preaching to the clusters of passers-by huddled around them.

As they made their way along the riverbank, they came upon a larger crowd. About thirty people stood around something Joshua couldn't quite see, so he jostled forward to get a closer look. Peering through the spectators, he saw an elderly man sitting cross-legged on the ground with a flute in his mouth. He was playing music and shifting his head from side to side. In front of him was a small, barrel-shaped wicker basket. Everyone was staring at it. Standing beside the flute player was another man. He was fat and wore lots of gold chains around his neck. The fat man made his way around the basket, addressing the onlookers.

"And now, my friends," he said, wafting his arms about like a showman, "behold how the one and only Wadjet tamer in the entire Kingdom of Edufu will call forth the dark beast."

He tiptoed around the musician while gesturing to the basket. His eyes were wide as if directing everyone to watch something incredible about to happen.

A hissing sound came from the basket. The crowd fell silent. The old man on the ground continued to play his flute and sway his head. Then a black snake's head peered up out of the basket. A second one joined it. The crowd gasped. Everyone took a step back.

"Do not be afraid, my friends," the showman said in a low voice with even more flamboyant hand gestures.

The two black heads danced around each other, staring at the musician. The snake had several red rings around its body. Both heads had shiny black tongues that darted in and out, flapping.

There was a snapping sound, and a Kimalla appeared right beside Andrew. He ignored it at first, but the cute animal stood up onto its back limbs and whimpered up at him with wide green eyes. It was a scrawny looking creature with scratches on its body like it had been in a fight and lost. It looked hungry. Andrew reached into his pocket and pulled out a small piece of River Palm fruit. The Kimalla's eyes widened. It tugged at Andrew's leg, licking its lips. Andrew bent down and handed the fruit to the little animal, which took the food and then disappeared.

"Be careful, my friend," a woman in the crowd said to Andrew. "Don't let them bite you, or you will get sick."

"Thanks," Andrew said. He smiled politely.

"Kimallas aren't the only things to be afraid of here," she said. She nodded toward the fat man, who was still working the crowd with his flamboyant routine.

"You mean the snakes?" Sarah asked.

"Well, it is true the bite from the Wadjet *will* kill, but those aren't the only *snakes* in Ramanna." Once again, she gestured at the fat man, now making his was around the crowd with a hat. People were throwing coins into it. The woman walked away before the man reached her.

As the crowd dispersed, the fat man collected the last coin before putting the lid back onto the wicker basket. He then tossed two small coins to the old man with the flute, stuffing all the larger ones into his own pocket.

"Come on," Joshua said, "let's check out the temple."

He led the others through the streets, making their way towards the temple. It wasn't hard to find. The obelisk was the tallest structure for miles around, visible from everywhere in the city.

They stumbled upon a large, rectangular courtyard. In the centre at one end stood the obelisk. It was as tall as the statue at the front of the temple in Asteena and no less impressive. The golden-yellow monument was flat on all four sides, tapering to a point at the top. Strange symbols were carved on each side. Hundreds of them covered the structure, stretching all the way to the top on three sides, but the bottom section of the fourth surface was bare. Chisel marks obscured the carvings there.

There was a hole right through the obelisk near the top. A bulbous pane of glass filled it. Sunlight passing through the lens cast a bright light onto the ground below.

Along each side of the courtyard, a series of statues stood on stone plinths. Each depicted the same regal figure, of a muscular man wearing a skirt and a headdress, similar to the monument at the temple of Asteena. They held different poses, hands stretched out towards the hole near the top of the obelisk.

Down at the far end of the courtyard was a flat building with a row of stone steps leading to a grand arched door. In the centre of the door was a round opening. There were no windows anywhere on the building, but more carvings depicting the same regal figure decorated the stone front on either side of the door.

"Welcome to the great temple of Ramanna, my friends," came a voice from behind them.

Joshua spun around. An old man stood there smiling with his arms folded into his robe. He had white hair, but something else was odd. One of his eyes was blue, the other green.

"I see you have been admiring the temple," he said in a warm and welcoming tone.

"We were just looking at it," Joshua said. "Can you tell us, who are all these statues of?"

"This is our great leader. His Divine Majesty King Ahmoses, the third of his name."

The man tapped his chest with the palm of his hand and bowed.

"And that?" Joshua asked, turning to the obelisk.

"This is the Eye of Tekhenu."

"The what?" Andrew asked.

The man smiled at Andrew. "When the sun sets, the eye shines into the temple."

He nodded at the arched door with the hole in the middle. The ball of light cast by the glass pane halfway up the obelisk was transiting across the stone steps.

"What happens when the light reaches the doorway?" Sarah asked.

The man smiled at her warmly. "Here," he walked towards the obelisk. "The story is written. See?"

He removed one hand from under his robe and gestured to the carvings on the sides of the obelisk as he read the strange symbols carved into the stone structure.

Christopher D. Morgan

The Eye of Tekhenu guides the path to true enlightenment.
May it see into your soul.
What was lost will be found.
It lights the path to the afterlife for Her Holiness The Divine Majesty Queen Raha.
She who commands the forces of nature.
The magic of the Divine Majesty Queen Raha rests with her.
He who discovers the orb may command…

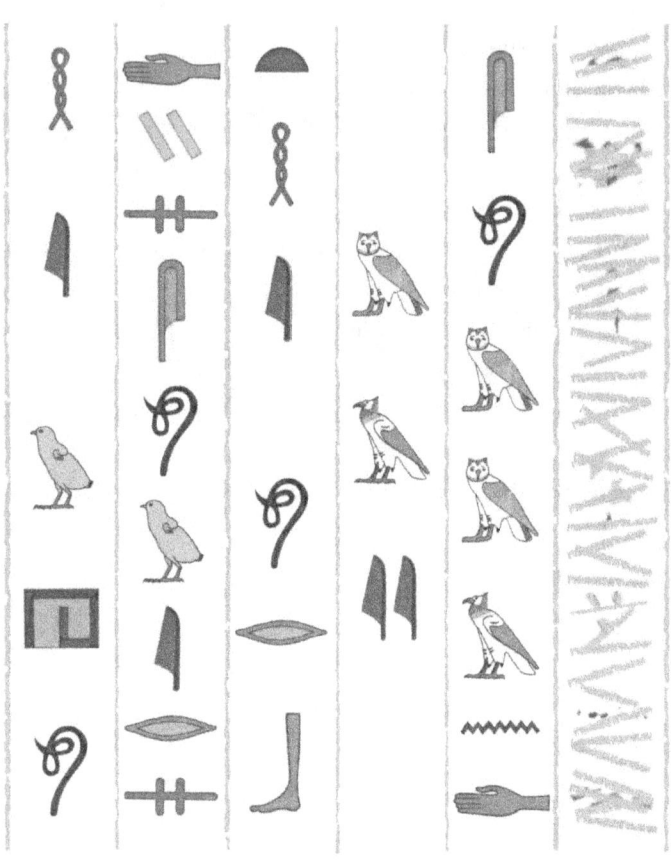

He then stopped reading, turned and smiled at them all again.

"Well, what happens to 'he who discovers the orb', then?" Andrew pressed. "What can he command?"

"Nobody knows," the man said brushing his hand over the blank section of the obelisk. "Many centuries ago, a war raged throughout the Valley of Edufu. Many ancient artefacts were damaged, including The Eye of Tekhenu. There is no written record of the last part of the story."

"And who is this Queen Raha?" Sarah asked.

The man held his hand to a particular carving. It was an elongated oval with four symbols within it.

"This," he added, pointing to the elongated oval, "is Her Divine Majesty Queen Raha. She was one of the most powerful rulers of Edufu. For over fifty years she reigned."

"Could we look inside?" Joshua asked.

"Of course," the man said warmly. "Come, I will show you."

He led them down the courtyard between the statues and up the steps to the front of the temple. He pushed the great arched door open.

Inside was a small chamber. At the back was a stone altar with a golden pyramid atop it. Joshua recognised it right away. It was just like the pyramid they had seen inside the Temple of Asteena. They walked up to the platform. At the apex of the pyramid was a shallow recess. Joshua's eyes widened. It would fit the Orb of Memory they had taken from the Temple of Asteena.

"Please," the man said kindly, "feel free to spend as much time here as you like. It is time for me to pray." He tipped his head forward and walked through a door to the side of the altar.

Once the man was out of sight, Joshua could barely contain his excitement. "We should come back here at sunset when the light shines through the hole in the door."

Andrew and Sarah nodded in agreement, and they left the temple.

CHAPTER TWELVE
The Half Man

"How long do we have?" Joshua asked Sarah. She looked at the sun and ball of light still transiting up the steps of the temple.

"Hmm. I'd say we have another couple of hours yet."

Just then, a Kimalla popped into view. It was the same scrawny-looking animal Andrew had fed earlier. It stood on its hind limbs and whimpered at Andrew again.

"Looks like you have made a new friend," Sarah chuckled.

Andrew crouched down, pulled out another piece of fruit and held it out in the palm of his hand. The scruffy-looking Kimalla sniffed before snatching the fruit. Once again, it disappeared with a snap.

"Come on," Joshua suggested. "We should try to keep a low profile."

They walked off into the side streets to find somewhere quiet.

Instead, they stepped into a hubbub of activity. A queue of people lined up to enter a building behind the temple. A man at the front of the queue ushered them through a door, collecting coins from each.

"That's it, my friends, step right up. Don't be shy. A gift from the gods is he. Nothing like it will you find anywhere in the

Valley of Edufu. Come, ladies and gentlemen, that's right, step forward. Good fortune will find those that touch the head of the half-man."

Joshua was leading Andrew and Sarah away from the crowd at first, but the words *half-man* resonated with him, and he stopped. The row of people shuffling into the small building piqued his curiosity.

"What is it?" Sarah asked.

"I'm not sure. Let's check that out."

"I thought you said to keep a low profile," Andrew said.

"Yeah, I know. It's just...I don't know. That man said something about a...half-man. I wonder if..."

They walked towards where the queue of people shuffled along the wall, then the group made their way around to the side away from the crowd. There was a window there, just low enough for them to reach. They stood on tiptoe and peered through.

Inside, there was a small hall with a line of people being led one at a time towards a little man sitting on a chair. One by one, they touched the short man's head before being ushered away.

"That's...that's Galleon," Joshua said to the other two.

"What's he doing here?" Andrew asked.

"Maybe he's in the same boat we are," Sarah suggested. "You know, with no memories of who he is or where he came from."

"He looks happy enough," Andrew chuckled.

"We can't just leave him here," Joshua said.

Galleon noticed the three of them peering through the window. He squinted at them. Then he stood and said something to the man ushering people to and from the line. The man gestured for him to sit back down. Galleon frowned, yelled at him and strode out of sight. Moments later, he appeared from around the corner.

"Galleon!" Joshua called out to him, trying at the same time to be as quiet as possible. "Over here! Quickly!" He whispered loudly.

Galleon walked up to them. "I know you. You're...damn it. It's on the tip of my tongue..."

"Joshua," Joshua whispered at him through raised eyebrows.

"That's it! You're Joshua."

"Shhh," Joshua said, putting his finger to his mouth.

Galleon frowned at them. "All of you look...somehow familiar."

"What *do* you remember, Galleon?" Sarah whispered.

"Galleon? Is my name Galleon? Oh. But they told me it was Halfman. In fact, they told me lots of strange things—none of which have made much sense, if I'm honest."

"Your name is Galleon. You're our friend. Those people inside? They're just trying to take advantage of you," Joshua said, looking back over his shoulder.

"I don't understand," Galleon shook his head.

"What's the last thing you do remember clearly?" Sarah asked.

"Well," Galleon scratched his head. "I woke up, not far from here, I think...not sure how long it was. Yesterday? Yes, I think it was yesterday. It might have been the day before? I don't know. It's all still a bit hazy. Anyway, I had no idea where I was or who I was. The next thing I know, people are lining up to touch my bloody head. Can you believe it? I'm not sure, but they seem to think I'm some god or something. I was brought here and have been sitting in that small hall ever since. People have been coming and going, all wanting a piece of this," he tapped the top of his head with his hand.

"It's the memory barrier. It wiped all of our memories when we arrived here," Joshua whispered.

"Don't be so bloody stupid. I'm sure I'd remember something like that happening. Honestly!"

Andrew laughed. "At least he hasn't lost his charming wit and amazing intellect," he whispered to Joshua.

"Come on, we have to get you out of here," Joshua said.

"But—"

"No buts! We'll explain everything later. Come on, before they realise you're gone. They're making a fortune out of you, and they aren't going to like it if you leave."

Joshua led Galleon and the others away from the building when…

"HEY!" The man Galleon yelled at in the hall came running out of the building towards them. Two more charlatans followed, both shouting.

"Quickly! RUN!" Joshua shouted.

The group sprinted through back alleys trying to evade the pursuing charlatans. Rounding a corner, Joshua spotted a small building similar to the storage room he and Sarah first woke up in when they arrived in the Valley of Edufu.

"In here. Quickly!" He opened the door and hastened everyone inside. Once they were all in, he shut the door behind him. Moments later, footsteps ran past.

CHAPTER THIRTEEN
A Message from the King

Convinced the charlatans had lost them and weren't coming back, Joshua and the others sat down.

"Right," Galleon said, "I need to know more about what's going on. You say we're all good friends, but I only have vague memories of you. You do look familiar, but my mind has been playing tricks on me lately."

"Your confusion is perfectly understandable, Galleon," Sarah said. "This world has a barrier that removes memories of anyone that passes through it."

"But I don't remember—"

"You don't remember much at the moment because your memory has been altered," Sarah persisted.

"But it's okay. We've found a way to get our memories back," Joshua said.

Galleon narrowed his eyes. "And what exactly are we doing in this place then?"

Nobody knew what to tell him.

"Well, to be honest," Joshua heaved a big sigh, "we're not entirely sure ourselves. Apparently, I have some important memories that the king needs."

"The king?" Galleon said, with more than a hint of scepticism.

"That's right," Joshua nodded.

"And just exactly how do you know all of this if you've lost all your memories?" Galleon folded his arms as though to suggest he'd found a flaw in Joshua's fantastic tale.

"Well, we met someone in another city south of here. He's working for the king and...he told us." Joshua's voice tapered off as he realised how unconvincing this might all sound.

"And you believed him," Galleon said, now staring at Joshua through raised brows.

"Um...yes," Joshua said, somewhat unconvincingly.

"So I should *not* believe the people here telling *me* things, but *you* should believe some *stranger* telling you fantastic things. Is that about right? Hmm? Honestly!"

Joshua looked at Sarah, hoping she might know some other way to convince Galleon.

"Oh, the papyrus, remember?" she said.

"Yes!" Joshua exclaimed with wide eyes. "The king sent us a message." He removed the rolled-up piece of papyrus from his keeper bag to show the message to Galleon. Then his shoulders sank as he remembered. "Only, the message disappeared again."

Galleon continued his unconvinced stare. "So, what you're saying is that you have a blank piece of paper, right?"

Joshua wafted the roll of papyrus at Galleon saying, "Look, everything we've been telling you is the truth."

Sarah squinted at the papyrus in Joshua's hand. "Hold on a moment. Joshua, open it up. There's something there."

Everyone watched Joshua unroll the papyrus. His eyes lit up at the sight of a new message.

Hello Joshua. I am pleased to see you are at least still alive…for now. I am hoping you have found the Orb of Memory and you have used it well. With any luck, you will have made it to Ramanna. You possess something that is of great value to me — to us all. Time is running out. It may soon be too late. The Orb of Wind could bring you to me sooner. It once resided in Ramanna. Alas, I fear it has been lost to time. I pray you will make it to me soon here in the capital city of Astowan, and that what was taken from you will be returned by the time you are here.

- Yours as always, His Divine Majesty, King Ahmoses III

Joshua read the message a second time. He then showed the others, who took turns studying it.

"What's this Orb of Memory?" Galleon asked. His scepticism had all but evaporated.

Joshua reached into his keeper bag and pulled out the clear crystal and handed it to Galleon.

The Imp held it up to his face, running his finger across it. "This looks very familiar. I'm sure I've seen something like this before."

"We all do, too," Joshua said. "We took this from the Temple of Asteena, but not before we used it to recover some of our memories."

"Is that what it does? Restore memories?"

Joshua nodded. "Only *some* of our memories have returned, though. Jafar told us to use the Orb of Memory at each of five temples. Hopefully, by the time we reach Astowan, we'll get all our memories back."

"And then what?" Galleon asked.

Joshua shook his head. He pointed to the papyrus in Sarah's hands. "The king wants one of the memories I have. What that memory is and what its significance is, I really couldn't say."

"What's this Orb of Wind?" Sarah asked, looking up from the papyrus. "The Orb of Wind could bring you to him sooner. I wonder what he means by that?"

Joshua shook his head.

Just at that moment, the same scrawny-looking Kimalla Andrew had already fed twice appeared.

Galleon didn't take the sudden occurrence of an animal popping into existence out of thin air very well. The shock sent the Imp springing backwards, knocking his head.

"Ouch! What's that?" He shouted, pushing himself hard against the wall as though trying to escape.

"Relax! Don't worry. It won't harm you." Andrew reached out to pat the Kimalla on the head. "You're not going to harm anyone are you, little fella?"

The Kimalla looked up at Andrew, begging for more treats. Andrew scratched it under its chin, and it half closed its eyes, making a purring sound.

"These are Kimallas," Sarah said. "They pop in and out all the time here. This one seems to have taken a liking to Andrew."

"Do they talk?" Galleon asked, his sarcasm still intact.

Under any other circumstances, this would be a silly question, but with everything else they had experienced since arriving here, it wasn't such an odd thing to ask.

"No," Joshua said. "Well, not that we know of. We haven't seen any talking Kimallas yet, at least."

"Oh, well, that's a pity. Otherwise, we could have asked *it* where to find the Orb of Wind."

The Kimalla stood up on its two back feet and jumped up and down squealing.

"I think it's hungry again, Andrew," Joshua said.

"No, hold on," Sarah said. "It became agitated when Galleon said Orb of Wind."

Once again, the Kimalla squealed. It leapt to the door, staring at the handle.

"It's trying to tell us something," Sarah exclaimed. "Andrew, open the door!"

Andrew pushed the door open, and the Kimalla leapt through.

"Quickly," Joshua said. "Let's see where it goes."

Once outside, Joshua and the others followed the agile Kimalla as it leapt between the buildings. It led them through the back streets, stopping now and then to let them catch up.

Panting from their exertions, they found themselves behind a derelict out-of-the-way building several streets away from the temple. The dilapidated structure was ancient. It was in such a state of disrepair, it might come tumbling down around them.

The Kimalla disappeared inside. Making sure nobody saw them, Joshua and the others followed.

Christopher D. Morgan

CHAPTER FOURTEEN

The Tomb of Queen Raha

Inside, there were cobwebs everywhere, along with a layer of dust so thick it was hard to see anything at all. The stone building had no upstairs. The half-rotten ceiling joists, riddled with little holes, looked like they might collapse at any moment.

Andrew was the last to enter, pushing the door closed behind him, causing dust to fall from the beams that barely held up the roof. The Kimalla leapt across the room, bouncing off dusty old chairs and tables. It stopped over by the wall, scratching at the floor.

Joshua wiped away the thick layer of dust from the floor by the animal. "Here, come and have a look at this."

Sarah knelt beside him. She leaned forward and blew hard. Dust flew everywhere, sending Joshua into a fit of coughing. Sarah felt the surface with her fingers. There was a slight recess in the floor. She followed the groove around, blowing away the dust as she went, revealing a complete rectangle. Wiping more dust away, she found a metal ring about the size of her hand recessed into the stone. She pulled on it.

"It's stuck," she said. "Here, help me with this."

Joshua and Andrew both grabbed the ring and yanked hard. The slab dislodged and lifted at a hinge from one end. Andrew raised it to reveal a stairway leading down into a dark hole. The Kimalla leapt in and disappeared. Joshua climbed into the hole and down the steps. Everyone else followed.

They found themselves in a damp tunnel. There were echoes of water dripping from the ceiling every few paces. The walls were rough as if the passage had been dug by hand. The ground was uneven and wet. They walked along the shaft through ankle-deep water, following the sound of the Kimalla as it bounced back and forth off the walls ahead of them. Every few paces, cracks in the ceiling allowed thin slivers of light through.

They crept along for about half an hour before the Kimalla stopped. It jumped up and down several times next to a section of tunnel wall that was smooth. An object stuck out from the wall as if placed there deliberately. It was a smooth, rectangular, stone slab. It looked out of place.

Joshua tried to push the obstruction but wasn't able to dislodge it. "Andrew, see if we can move whatever this is out of the way."

Andrew and Joshua both leaned into the slab with their shoulders. They pushed as hard as they could from one side. It creaked as it rubbed against the tunnel wall, revealing an opening. They shifted it far enough to squeeze through into a small chamber. Thin shards of light came through tiny cracks in the ceiling.

"I think we're beneath the temple." Sarah looked up through the cracks.

The chamber was barely big enough to stand in. In the centre was a large, rectangular stone slab.

Sarah ran her hands over the top and sides of it. "It looks like this top part is a lid," she whispered. "Hey, there are markings here. These symbols are similar to those on the Eye of Tekhenu."

"What, you mean that tall pointy thing in front of the temple?" Andrew asked.

Sarah nodded. "Here! Look!" She brushed away a layer of dust and then blew hard, revealing a series of carved symbols. "Look at this!"

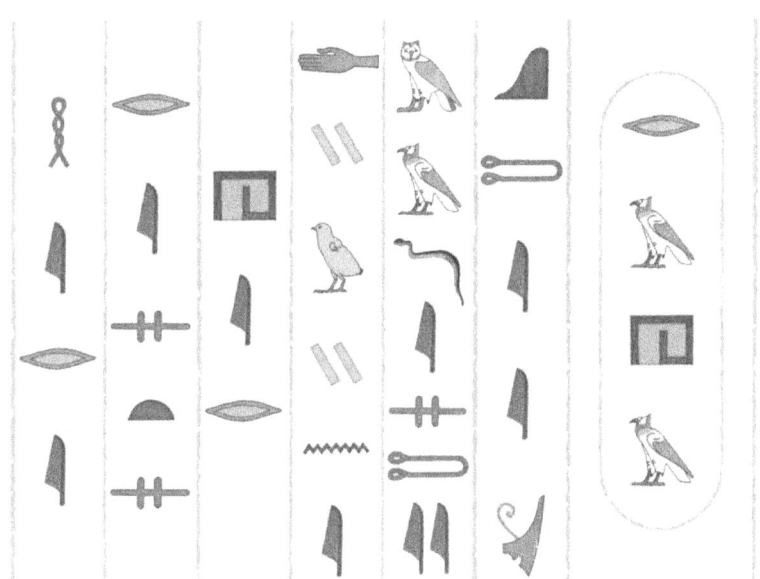

Sarah pointed to an elongated oval enclosing four symbols. "This is the symbol for Queen Raha. Remember? When the priest at the temple read the writing on the Eye of Tekhenu? He said this symbol represented Queen Raha."

Sarah tried to remember the story. "The magic of the queen rests with her," she whispered. "That's what the priest said when he was reading the story, I'm sure of it."

"So if this is her tomb," Joshua said, "then this is..."

"This is where the magic resides," Sarah gasped with wide eyes. "This is where the Orb of Wind is."

The Kimalla again jumped up and down, squealing.

"And he who *finds* the magic may command...something," Andrew said.

"Well?" Galleon spoke up for the first time since entering the tunnel. "What are we waiting for? Let's open it up and find out."

Joshua and Andrew pushed the lid, heaving it aside. The stone slab scraped as it slid open.

Once the lid was half off, they stopped pushing. Everyone looked inside. It was a hollow box with a long, body-shaped object inside, wrapped in layers of bandages.

"Whoa," Andrew gasped.

"That's a corpse," Sarah whispered.

On top of the wrapped body was a clear crystal. Joshua picked it up and blew the dust from it. It was just like the Orb of Memory, but the carving on the side was different. Instead of the form of a human head, there were lines with loops at one end.

"Those must represent the wind," Joshua said. "We've found it," he beamed with a gasp. "This is the Orb of Wind."

Sarah screamed as a black snakehead burst through the face of the wrapping around the corpse, quickly followed by another. When the two snakes emerged fully, it revealed itself to be a single, two-headed Wadjet. Another burst through the corpse's abdomen. Soon Wadjets were emerging from every corner of the mummy. The small chamber echoed with the deafening sound of snakes. They slithered up the wall of the tomb and onto the chamber floor.

"Quickly! RUN!" Joshua shouted.

Everyone hurried out of the chamber and back into the tunnel with Wadjets slithering out after them. They sprinted as best they could through the dark tunnel. Dozens of the venomous snakes followed them the whole way. Exhausted and panting, they made it to the stone steps leading into the derelict building.

Joshua helped everyone up. "Hurry! We have to get out of here!"

Everything around them rumbled. The building shook with dust falling from the ceiling. Galleon was the last one to be pulled up. Joshua ran after him, pushing him out of the building, which was now collapsing all around them. He dove through the door just in time to avoid being crushed as the entire structure collapsed into a pile of debris and rubble behind him.

The noise of the collapse was deafening. Joshua lay there as dust fell all around him. Then, everything was silent.

Christopher D. Morgan

CHAPTER FIFTEEN
The Orb of Wind

Sarah helped Joshua to his feet and brushed him down.

"Hey, look!" Andrew exclaimed, pointing at the Eye of Tekhenu.

With the sun close to setting, a much more intense beam of light shone through the hole in the obelisk.

"Quickly," Joshua cried, "we don't have much time before the sun's light enters the temple."

Everyone raced after Joshua as he made his way through the back streets. By the time they arrived, a circular beam of light was moving up the arched door.

Joshua sprinted up the stone steps, and they all followed him in. As he ran across the hall, he reached into his keeper bag and pulled out the Orb of Memory.

"Hurry! Everyone behind the altar!" he shouted, fumbling to place the transparent crystal atop the golden pyramid.

The hole in the door brightened. As it did, an unmistakable sound rang out all around them. Chills ran down Joshua's spine as horror coursed through his veins. Wadjets slithered towards them from all directions. More followed behind those. They emerged from every corner—even up through cracks in the floor.

The rays of light coming through the hole in the door continued to intensify. Two Wadjets had made it onto the altar and approached the golden pyramid. Sarah screamed, her hand shooting to her mouth.

There was a blinding flash of light as the beam struck the Orb of Memory. A blue halo surrounded the orb. Shards of brilliant white light emanated from it in all directions. It lit up the surrounding chamber so much that everyone had to shield their eyes. All the Wadjets squealed, turning away from the brightness.

Moments later, the beam moved away from the orb and dimmed. The halo disappeared, and the chamber was once again dark. The ball of light now transited up the back wall.

Joshua's eyes adjusted to the dark again after a few seconds. "Is everyone okay?" he asked, panting.

They all nodded.

"Well," Galleon said, "if that doesn't clean your sinuses I don't know what would. Honestly!"

The lifeless bodies of dozens of Wadjets littered the chamber.

"Are they dead?" Sarah asked.

Joshua shook his head. "I'm not sure."

He walked around the altar to the centre of the room where several Wadjets lay motionless on the floor. He crouched down and jabbed at one with his finger. It wasn't moving. Very slowly he reached down to pick it up. The two heads and tail hung draped across his hand. The smooth, scaly skin was cold.

"Yeah, I think they're all dead," Joshua said. He held one head up to his face. Both eyes glistened. Joshua gently pushed the snake's lower jaw down, revealing two needle-like fangs.

The Wadjet's mouth suddenly burst open, hissing at Joshua. He leapt back, dropping the reptile and stumbling to the floor. Every Wadjet burst into life, generating a loud hiss that echoed around the room. They all slithered towards Joshua, who was kicking them away as he tried to push himself backwards with his heels.

A larger Wadjet slithered between Joshua's legs. It was almost upon him when Andrew's boot came flying across Joshua's vision, kicking the Wadjet clear across the chamber.

"Grab my hand!" Andrew yanked Joshua to his feet. Joshua and Andrew kicked several more Wadjets across the floor. The snakes were lunging at them with their mouths wide open, exposing two long fangs protruding from their upper jaws.

"Quickly!" Andrew shouted, "Let's get out of here!"

He ran towards the door, kicking Wadjets as he went, sending them flying, clearing just enough of a path for the others to dash for it. They all tore to the arched door. Outside, they ran down the stone steps and away from the temple.

Joshua glanced over his shoulder. Dozens—perhaps hundreds—of Wadjets slithered out into the courtyard. "Come on," he shouted, "to the boat!"

With the sound of hissing chasing after them, they ran as fast as they could. Screams rang out everywhere as countless Wadjets flooded the city streets. It was pandemonium, with mobs of people running in all directions trying to escape the onslaught of the venomous snakes.

Joshua led them down the riverbank and onto the felucca. More Wadjets kept chasing. There were tens of thousands of them, like a vast black blanket smothering the cobblestone streets and buildings. People screamed as they tried to flee, but there was nowhere for them to go. The Wadjets were everywhere.

The group clambered onto the boat. Andrew struggled to lower the sail. The tangled rope securing it in place wouldn't loosen. A stream of Wadjets slithered up the walkway, hissing and thrashing their heads.

"Quickly Andrew! NOW!"

"I can't get it loose! It's stuck!" Andrew screamed.

Joshua then had an idea. He pulled out the Orb of Wind and held it out in front of him. Nothing happened. The Snakes were now on the boat, dozens of them crawling along the side rail. Then Joshua blew at the orb.

There was a sudden build-up of turbulent air behind the felucca. The wind turbulence intensified, propelling the boat through the water at high speed. Joshua and the others had to grab hold of something to stop being swept overboard. The sail dropped into place, and the boat raced up the river at a blistering pace. The banks flew past them like a blur. All the snakes flew out into the whirling air, landing in the river.

All at once, it was over. The gust of wind stopped, bringing the felucca to a splashing halt. The front of the boat dipped into the water, sending a huge wave outwards on both sides. Everyone stumbled as the rear of the vessel crashed down. Jafar's felucca bobbed up and down a few times before coming to rest. The sail flapped in the last breaths of the dying wind.

Christopher D. Morgan

CHAPTER SIXTEEN
More Memories Returned

After the wind had died down, Joshua remained clinging to the base of the mast a little longer, his arms wrapped all the way around it, his heart still pounding and his eyes closed. The Orb of Wind remained clenched in his hand.

Now that calm had again descended, he peered around. The surrounding waters were devoid of any turbulence other than a few ripples caused by the boat coasting in the light wind. A warm breeze engulfed him like a blanket. When he opened his eyes fully, a patchwork of fields stretched out along both banks of the river all the way to the mountain ranges on the horizon. The setting sun cast a pleasant, warm glow onto the calm waters.

Andrew was at the aft of the boat, releasing his tight grip on the rudder and struggling to his feet. There was no sign of the obelisk or anything else—just endless fields and a ridge of white-tipped mountains in the distance on either side.

"Is everyone okay?" Sarah asked, stumbling to her feet, untying a rope she had wrapped around her arm.

"I think so," Joshua nodded. "Where's Galleon?"

A muffled knocking sound resounded from a barrel lashed to the side rail.

"Will somebody get me out of here!"

Two feet poked out the top, thrashing in the air.

"I think we found him." Andrew untied the barrel and pushed it over.

"Ouch!" Galleon slid out and picked himself up off the deck. "Andrew, was that bloody necessary?" the Imp complained, brushing himself down. He turned to Joshua. "Those bloody orbs of yours will be the death of me. Honestly!"

"All those snakes," Sarah shook her head with a grave look on her face. "Where did they come from? There must have been tens of thousands of them. Those people didn't stand a chance."

Joshua shook his head. "I don't know, but I bet the Goat had something to do with it." Joshua's eyes widened as the realisation hit him. "Hey, can anyone else remember the Goat now?"

"I can," Andrew said.

"Yeah, me too," Galleon nodded. "I remember seeing him once. That was also thanks to another one of your bloody orbs, Joshua."

Sarah also nodded. "I can remember him now. I mean, I don't know what he looks like. I don't think I've ever seen him before. But I know we've all been running from him. What else can you remember, Joshua?"

Joshua stared into the distance. "He's trying to kill me," he said in a slow, contemplative tone. "He has been for a while now. I *think* he's afraid of me." Joshua sighed, unable to think of anything else.

"Perhaps the reason he's afraid has to do with why the king wants you?" Sarah suggested. "Jafar said the king had been at war with the Goat, remember? Maybe you know something about how to defeat the Goat, and the king is hoping to learn what that is."

"Who's Luana?" Galleon asked. "I have a memory of someone called Luana."

Joshua remembered the feather they had found when he and Sarah first arrived here. "She's from some other place. I don't know where exactly, or what I mean by that," he shook his head with a look of frustration on his face. "At least…she wasn't from here."

"Wasn't?" Galleon asked.

Joshua's face changed as he recalled a harrowing memory. "I think…she's dead."

"Islands," Andrew said, thinking hard. "She was from a place where there were lots of islands. And crabs—"

"Archipelago," Sarah said.

"Archi-what? Andrew looked perplexed.

"Archipelago," she repeated. "That's where Luana was from—a world of islands."

Joshua nodded.

"So, it, um, seems that we're all good friends, then." Galleon said, bouncing on his feet. "I, um," he giggled. "I guess I should, um, apologise for my behaviour back there. I mean, I should never have questioned you. I'm sorry about that."

"Don't worry, mate," Andrew chuckled, patting his friend on the shoulder. "I'll fill you in on everything you need to know. You do remember you do all my cooking and cleaning for me, right?"

"Hmm. Something tells me that particular memory will never come back to me. But I *can* remember how loud you snore."

Andrew and Galleon both laughed.

The Goat sneered down at His latest victim lying on the floor of His dark lair. He snorted at the man's unwillingness to talk. Steam shot from the Goat's nostrils each time He exhaled. His arms hung out by his sides. They pushed away from his body by the sheer mass of His muscular torso and the thickness of his biceps. One forearm was missing, bone protruding from its end. In the centre of His chest was a gaping wound. The vicious half-creature kept His dark eyes fixed on the wretched man curled up before Him as He paced back and forth, waiting for the old man to crack from the strain.

"What has the boy told you about the Portallas?" He screamed down at the whimpering wreck.

Jafar looked up at a blurred vision of the Goat. He could scarcely see anything through his puffed and bruised eyes. All he could make out was a hazy and indistinct silhouette of his tormentor looming over him.

The frail old man's body was already showing signs of giving out. He had lost count of the number of hours he had been here, being tortured by the Goat. His shattered left arm and both legs left him unable to move. Burn marks covered his entire body, and he had knife wounds to his head and neck. Blood oozed from the tips of his fingers.

"Tell me what I want to know, old man! If the boy's memories are restored by the time he reaches Astowan, I swear you will remain here for the rest of your days while I torture you day and night. Now tell me! Or must I remove more fingernails? Hmm? TELL ME NOW!"

The Goat's terrifying scream echoed around the dark room.

Jafar struggled to inhale a lungful of air. The intense pain of the multiple shattered ribs made it a chore. Each breath was an uphill marathon.

The Goat shook His head violently. He looked up into the dark vaulted ceiling and howled.

Moments later, a rattling sounded in the distance, getting louder. The noise reverberated around the dark lair. Something substantial approached. The rattling noise encircled the Goat, just beyond the light.

Then a giant snake emerged from the darkness. It was twice the thickness of an adult human. The beast was black down its entire length. Huge scales shimmered all along its back and sides. It raised its head high off the ground, revealing a deep shade of red to its underbelly. Two shiny black eyes—each bigger than a fist—perched atop the snake's head. A long, thick, black tongue shot out of the creature's mouth and whipped up and down several times.

"The boy is heading north," the Goat said to the snake. "He will soon be in Alexur."

The snake's enormous head nodded as if to acknowledge the Goat's words.

"I want you to kill them," the vile creature said. He lowered His head and peered at the snake through His thick bushy eyebrows. "I want you to kill them all."

The Goat leered at Jafar, who quivered on the floor in a pool of blood, and continued in a low cackle, "starting with this one."

The snake slithered around the room, making a full circle. It doubled back and forth, coiling itself into a series of figure eights, before sliding right up to Jafar. The snake raised its head higher off the ground and pointed its nose towards the heap of flesh and bones by the Goat's feet.

Two streams of steaming fluid shot from the snake's nose. Jafar screamed in agony. The fluid hit the tortured old man's body, melting through his clothing and flesh. Steam rose from the burn marks. Parts of Jafar's body dissolved from the acid jets, exposing bone. Then the snake whipped its head down violently, sinking two enormous fangs into the broken man. When its head rose again, Jafar's body was no longer moving. He was no longer screaming. Jafar was dead.

A hideous grin spread across the Goat's face. The snake uncoiled itself and slithered into the dark recesses of the dank lair. The rattling noise faded until it was gone.

CHAPTER SEVENTEEN
The Slaughter of Alexur

It wasn't clear how far up the river the Orb of Wind had propelled them, but soon the outline of a city appeared in the distance. Once again, a large monument revealed the city's position long before anything else. Instead of an obelisk, this time it was the shape of a large, flattened snake's head poking up above the River Palms lining the banks. The structure shimmered yellow in the dwindling twilight.

Andrew joined Joshua at the stern of the boat. He let out a deep sigh. "Not more snakes. That's all we need."

Joshua stared at the snake looming on the horizon. "I wonder what this city is called."

"I wonder what'll try to kill us," Andrew snorted.

"There's a lot of smoke coming from this place." Sarah joined them. She pointed at dark grey plumes rising above the city skyline.

With light fading fast, Andrew steered them towards a cluster of other boats moored along the river.

"That's strange," Joshua said, as Andrew tied off the boat.

"What's strange?" Galleon asked.

"Where is everyone?"

"Well, it is getting dark. Maybe everyone is inside somewhere?"

There was a distant scream.

"I have a bad feeling about this." Joshua shook his head.

They disembarked and walked from the dock towards the city buildings. A handful of trading carts lay abandoned in the streets. Some were lying on their sides with fruits and other goods littering the ground. Kimallas popped in and out, stealing the unattended food.

As they got closer, smoke rose from something lying in the street. A woman lay motionless on the ground. Joshua knelt to check her pulse. Her head fell to one side when he pushed on it. Sarah shot her hand to her mouth, gasping. Joshua stood up and backed away. Flesh from the woman's face was missing.

"What could have done this?" Joshua asked.

"Her arms, too," Andrew pointed at smouldering burns running from her shoulders to her wrists. The flesh had dissolved, revealing bare bone. There was no skin at all on one hand.

Another distant scream rang out. Someone was in absolute agony. Then the cry stopped.

"Over here," Galleon said. "There's more."

They walked on to find more smouldering bodies; all of them were dead, their flesh dissolved away in places.

In the fading light, doors swung in the breeze as if people had fled. As they continued into the city, it was the same sight everywhere. Bodies littered the streets.

Then a sound — someone whimpering — came from just ahead. Striding forward, Joshua tried to locate the source of the crying. He stopped at each body, looking for signs of life.

"Spread out," he said to the others.

Everyone wandered around, listening for the sound. More screams rang out from inside the city.

"Help me…" came a faint voice.

"Over here!" Galleon shouted. Joshua and the others ran over. It was an old woman. Her arms were smouldering, but she was still breathing. Joshua knelt down and cradled her.

"H-help m-me," the woman murmured, her breathing shallow.

"Water! Hurry!" Joshua looked up, pleading.

Andrew ran towards a nearby building and disappeared inside.

Sarah knelt beside the woman. "It's okay, it's okay," she said. "We're going to help you. Try not to move."

"K-killed t-them," the woman stammered, straining to get the words out. "It k-killed t-them a-all."

"What happened here?" Joshua asked.

The woman reached out. Most of her fingers had no flesh on them. A light flickered over the top of the buildings in the direction she pointed, as if a fire raged somewhere in the distance. A loud rattling sound came from that direction.

"It's c-coming. Get out w-while you s-still c-can. Go, now, before it's too—"

The woman sputtered, blood trickling from her mouth. She gasped a last lungful of air. Then she fell silent. Sarah felt the still woman's neck for a pulse. She glanced up at Joshua and shook her head.

Andrew came running back with a water sack.

"You're too late," Galleon said. "She's gone. It sounds like something is rampaging through the city. I bet that's what killed this woman and all these others."

Whatever made the rattling sound wasn't stationary. It had moved around them and was now coming from the river. It was closing in on them.

"Come on," Joshua urged. "Whatever that is, I don't think we want to be here when it shows up."

Joshua and the others ran away from the rattling sound as fast as they could.

CHAPTER EIGHTEEN
Queen Neferemu's Intentions

King Ahmoses III squinted through the small mirror of the Eye of Horentus.

"Damn it!" He shouted, throwing the wooden staff to the floor.

Queen Neferemu eyed her husband, licking her finger, with a smirk forming on her face. "What is it, my love?"

"The Goat, he is trying my patience. Who does he think he is to be playing these games with His Divine Majesty? And now this…this monster he has unleashed on the people of Alexur."

The king threw his arms in the air and paced around the throne room with a frown. He mumbled to himself, gesturing and staring at the floor as he strutted.

"He is nothing, my love," the queen dismissed. "You are the true ruler of this kingdom. It is you the people love. You are the one they look to in times of trouble."

"And tell me, my love, hmm?" The king turned to her with his eyebrows raised. "What good is a king that cannot protect his people? Hmm? Hmm?"

He continued his pacing around the room.

"What good indeed," the queen whispered to herself, looking disinterested.

"Hmm? What was that?"

"I said. 'What a good king you are indeed.' Oh, my darling, come and sit down. You are too tense. Here," she beckoned the agitated ruler to his throne. "It will do you no good to keep this tension inside of you. You must let me help you slice through it."

The king huffed. "It is like he is always one step ahead of me," the king complained, storming back to his throne. He sat down and rested his chin on his fist, sulking.

The queen smiled. She walked around the back of the throne, reached over and kneaded the king's shoulders.

"Oh, my darling," she said with a dramatic gasp of surprise, "this tension. I do not know how you do it. With all this *ruling* you have to do, poor thing. Here, my lover, let your queen help you."

She massaged her husband's shoulders. After a few moments, he closed his eyes and grunted his approval as his wife worked the tense muscles in his neck and back. His shoulders sank more with each sensual stroke of her probing fingers.

"That's it, my darling, that's much better," she said in a seductive tone.

The king kept his eyes closed as his relaxation deepened. His head drooped as if he might nod off altogether.

"That's good, just relax my darling," the queen's voice lowered further.

She continued working him over with one hand. The other slid down the back of the throne. Shifting a piece of velvet cloth to one side, she reached in and grasped something.

"That's good, my love," she said in a slow voice, rhythmically pressing against the king's neck.

The king groaned with his eyes closed. The queen raised her other hand. Clenched within it was an ornate gold-encrusted dagger. She continued distracting her husband with one hand, the other raising the blade above his head.

"No!" The king blurted, leaping from his throne.

The queen scrambled to jam the dagger back into the compartment behind the throne, shifting the fabric into place again with her palm.

"No, no, no! This will not do at all," he stormed over to a plinth by the windows. Upon it was a glass bell, beneath which lay a white plume. He lifted the protective container and took the feather. The king held it up to his eyes and let out a deep sigh. Laying it on his open palm, he watched as it turned green.

The king turned to the queen, still standing behind his throne. She smiled back at him coyly. Then a bird shriek sounded from the open window. Moments later, a beautiful golden falcon soared towards the window. It flapped at the opening before landing gracefully on the ledge. As the bird hopped into the throne room, it grew and changed shape. Within seconds, it had morphed into the slender figure of a woman.

"King Ahmoses," the woman bowed reverently.

"It is good to see you again, Philaena. Your beauty shines more than all the gold in Edufu." The king took the woman's hand and kissed it, maintaining eye contact with her.

Queen Neferemu pulled a scornful look, scowling at the woman. She cleared her throat as if to draw attention to herself. Philaena turned to her and bowed. "Queen Neferemu. A pleasure, as always."

The queen returned the courtesy, but it was a half-hearted attempt — enough to satisfy protocol.

"How may I serve the king today?" Philaena asked, turning her attention back to the king.

"The boy is halfway to Astowan," he said. "He has arrived in Alexur, but I fear for his safety now more than ever. The Goat has unleashed terror on the city. He will be unable to find what he needs there on his own. But there is one who can help him."

The king tilted his head forward, keeping his eyes fixed on the Metamorph.

"The Oracle," she nodded. "I will guide the boy. Let us both hope it is not too late."

Philaena took a step back and shrank. Wings sprouted from her shoulders. In a moment, the transformation was complete; the Metamorph was again a glorious golden falcon. It hopped onto the window ledge and sprang forward, falling into a graceful glide. The magnificent bird flapped its wings and soared away into the distance. A shrill call faded as it disappeared toward the horizon.

CHAPTER NINETEEN
The Attack at Alexur

Joshua and the others ran through the maze of narrow streets of Alexur, trying to keep a distance from the loud rattling sound. Screams echoed between the buildings. Each time, someone would cry out in agony and then fall silent moments later.

They found their way to the snakehead temple. A patchwork of curved blocks joined with no gaps to form the ancient building. The enormous monument took the shape of a scaly snake's body that looped back and then forward over itself — three layers of the body leading to a raised head. Atop the structure, the snake's head pointed to the river. Parts of the stonework crumbled from centuries of decay. It was over a thousand years old. Perched atop the head were two huge glass eyes. There was no visible entrance.

"Are you sure this is the right place, Joshua?" Galleon asked.

Joshua shook his head. "I don't know, but this *must* be it? There's nothing else we've come across that looks even remotely like it might be a temple."

"How are we going to get inside? There's no door," Andrew puffed.

The rattling sound intensified, closing in on their position. All around the snake temple were stone structures. To the left was a narrow passageway between the temple and the adjacent building.

"Maybe the entrance is at the back somewhere. Here, let's try this way." Joshua beckoned them all down the narrow passageway.

With dusk having set in, it was hard to see much detail down the small alley. At the far end, a wall joined the temple to the adjacent building. With no door in sight, it was a dead end.

Approaching the front of the alley was the source of the terrifying noise. An enormous black snake slithered past the temple's base. The beast's circumference was three times that of Joshua's chest. Its vast body was so long it looped back and forth three times in front of the structure.

Joshua's anxiety soared as panic coursed through his veins. They were trapped. He held his breath, his heart pounding in his chest. A hand reached for his. It was Sarah. She locked eye contact with him, one finger to her mouth.

In the distance, the snake's tail rose high into the sky over the tops of the buildings. The terrifying rattling sound was coming from its tip, which was whipping side to side so fast the entire tail end was a blur.

The reptile lifted its head off the ground, scanning back and forth. Down its underbelly, the black scaly skin gave way to a deep red colour. A scream near the temple drew its attention, and it spun in that direction, expelling two shots of steamy fluid through its nostrils. The cry turned from one of fear to one of agony. The torment lasted several seconds and then…silence.

Sarah gasped, shooting her hand to her mouth. The dark creature's head whipped around as it peered down the dark alley in their direction.

The beast raised its head still higher and shifted it sideways, trying to see down the alley. Uncoiling its body, it moved toward them. A slimy black tongue emerged from its mouth and whipped up and down with such ferocity, it cracked several times in the air before sucking back in. The serpent's tail rattled again. The dark beast sped up, sliding down the alleyway. Everyone stepped backwards, but the stone wall prevented their escape.

The beast reared its head high into the air—clear above the height of the temple. Without warning, two shots of liquid gushed from the monster's nose. Everyone scattered, attempting to dodge the oncoming streams.

Sarah let out an agonised scream as the acid struck her across the face and down one arm. Steam rose from those contact points as the toxic fluid melted away her flesh.

The tail rattled more. The creature raised its head and opened its mouth wide, revealing two body-length fangs, both dripping with venom.

As it poised to strike, a shrill bird call rang out overhead. The noise bounced between the two buildings as an enormous golden falcon came flying into the alley. It lunged at the eyes of the snake, latching on with both feet and flapping its wings. The reptile's head whipped from side to side as it struggled to rid itself of the talons gouging at its eyes.

The dark creature reversed back up the alley, thrashing its head. Chunks of stone came crashing down as the beast smashed into the walls. Once it was out in the open, its body coiled back and forth with the falcon still latched on. The massive serpent whipped its tail, raising its head high into the sky. The head pointed upwards, thrashing until it shook the falcon loose. It then slithered away down between two of the buildings opposite the temple and was soon out of sight.

The golden falcon flapped a few times before turning down the alley. It came gliding through to where Joshua and the others were huddled around Sarah, who was writhing in agony on the ground. It flapped its majestic golden wings as it glided in to land before them, standing at least as tall as any of them.

The bird changed shape right in front of them. Its wings receded and its feathers shrunk to nothing. Moments later, a woman stood before them.

Joshua stood there with his jaw dropped. The woman regarded Sarah, grasping at her face and screaming. Steam rose from her skin as the snake's acid dissolved her alive.

The woman knelt beside Sarah. She held one hand palm down with outstretched fingers over the girl's form and moved it back and forth along her length. As she did, a green glow lit up Sarah's body. It came from Sarah herself. As the woman continued, Sarah's wounds shrank. Her skin re-formed, covering the bone and filling in the gaps that had dissolved away. After a few moments, she stopped screaming. Her wounds kept shrinking. Soon they were gone.

The woman stopped moving her hand, holding it above Sarah. The green glow subsided. Sarah opened her eyes. The stranger had healed her.

CHAPTER TWENTY
Philaena

The woman extended a hand to Sarah and helped her to her feet.

Joshua looked at his girlfriend in disbelief, his mouth hung open and his eyes still wide.

"A-are y-you okay?" He stammered, running his hand across her cheek.

Sarah nodded. She turned to the stranger and said, "I-I owe you my life. Thank you."

The woman smiled at Sarah.

"What was that thing?" Galleon asked.

"Never mind about that. Who are you, and how did you do...that?" Andrew blurted with wide eyes, pointing to Sarah's now healed face.

"My name is Philaena."

"You can change into a bird and back?" Joshua marvelled.

"And you can heal?" Galleon added.

Philaena nodded. "I can take many forms. I am a Metamorph."

"A M-meta...what?" Andrew asked.

Philaena smiled again. She had a pleasant, reassuring way about her. "I understand your confusion. I am the last of my kind from this world."

Joshua's face turned pallid. He looked down at the ground, a mournful expression spreading across his face. He couldn't understand why, but a wave of grief flooded his mind. It was as if a painful memory in him had surfaced at hearing the words 'last of my kind', but he couldn't remember the details.

"*This* world?" Joshua asked. "Do you mean there are others of your kind in other worlds?"

Philaena wore a solemn look. "I do not know if there are others of my kind. It may be that I am the last anywhere."

"Where do you come from?" Joshua asked.

"There were once many of my kind. We lived for thousands of years in peace with the peoples of many worlds. But we have suffered at the hands of the Goat over the centuries. Very few of us survive."

Joshua's eyes lit up. "You know the Goat? I-I think he's trying to kill us."

"He is," the Metamorph nodded. "Your life is in grave danger. The Goat is a ruthless predator—evil and twisted."

"Who is he? I mean, where does he come from?"

"The Goat is a magical being that lives in a different realm, one that is connected to many worlds through the Portallas."

"Portallas?" Joshua asked, narrowing his eyes. "That sounds familiar. What is it?"

"A gateway of sorts. It once joined many worlds. Centuries ago, people were able to move between worlds using the Portallas gateway."

"*Were* able to?" Sarah asked.

"When the Goat first came to power, he sealed the Portallas in each world. It is a form of control. He is fiercely jealous of anyone that possesses any magical powers. The Metamorphs and many others with supernatural abilities were all but wiped out by the Goat. My people have been systematically eradicated over many centuries. A few of my race were able to survive by going into hiding in different worlds. Others were…not so fortunate." She stared into nothingness with a sombre look on her face.

"So, he doesn't want anyone to open the Portallas?" Joshua asked.

"He sees this as a threat to his dominance, and with good reason. The Goat's magical power is finite. Once exhausted, it cannot be replenished. Sealing a Portallas requires immense amounts of magic—power he no longer possesses. With the opening of each new gateway, the Goat's powers weaken, and he grows more vulnerable."

"Well, that's good, then, right?" Andrew asked.

"Perhaps, but he also grows more desperate, which makes him even more dangerous."

"And this is why he's willing to kill so many innocent people?" Joshua asked.

"If enough gateways are opened, his magical power will diminish to the point that he *might* be defeated. He will stop at nothing to prevent the Portallas gateways from being reopened. In different worlds, he has annihilated entire races—counted in tens of thousands of people—to prevent this from happening, leaving nothing but barren and desolate wastelands."

"So why is he so intent on killing me? I have no idea how to open the Portallas in this world. What threat do I pose to him?"

"The king believes you do have the knowledge. It was stripped from you when you entered this world—hidden but not lost forever. The king can see glimpses of other worlds through the Eye of Horentus."

"What's that?" Andrew asked.

"The Eye of Horentus is a magical mirror. Through it, the king has seen you open the Portallas in another world, Joshua. He hopes that you can restore enough of your memories to help him do the same in this world."

"Well, I've already started remembering things since we used the Orb of Memory. We were hoping to use it here in Alexur to restore more of them. We arrived from Ramanna earlier today, looking for the temple. We thought this was it," he gestured to the snake-shaped building next to them, "but we can't find our way in."

"There is no entrance to the Temple of Alexur."

Joshua frowned. "Well, how are we supposed to get in, then?"

"There is something—someone—who might be able to help."

Joshua's eyes widened. "Who is it?"

"It is the Oracle. I have been sent here by the king to guide you to her."

"Well, we're lucky you found us when you did," Sarah said. "A few seconds more and we might all have been killed."

Philaena smiled. "Come, we have a long journey ahead of us. We should leave right away."

"But...I thought we had to get into the temple." Joshua gestured to the adjacent building. "It's right here."

"That is true, but only the Oracle can grant entry to the temple. Come, we must hurry. It is not safe for me to be out in the open for too long. If the Goat learns of my presence in this world, my life will be in grave danger. Please, stand back."

Philaena took a few steps backwards and again changed shape. She bent down onto her hands and knees and grew longer. Two huge wings sprouted from her midsection and her limbs stretched. Her face elongated. Seconds later, the transformation was complete. A beautiful pure white mare with enormous wings now stood before them. The graceful animal bent its two front legs, lowering its shoulders.

Joshua turned to the others. "Well, come on, then. Everyone get on."

Christopher D. Morgan

CHAPTER TWENTY-ONE
Finding the Oracle

Joshua and Andrew helped Sarah and Galleon onto Philaena's back. Andrew jumped up next, pulling Joshua up to the front position. The Metamorph turned towards the end of the alley. She reared up onto her hind legs and came down into a trot. She sped to a canter and then a gallop. Within seconds, Philaena was racing down the alley. Everyone held onto the horse's mane, which ran down the length of its back.

Clearing the buildings, the feathered horse extended its mighty wings. The graceful animal lifted into the air, soaring over the top of the temple. The wind rushed through Joshua's hair. Philaena climbed steadily in a southerly direction, with the city of Alexur fast receding below.

The cityscape dropped below them as the river stretched like a dark scar on the ground leading away in both directions. Soon, the snake temple of Alexur was but a small dot on the landscape below.

Philaena changed course, veering off to the east across the winding river. Joshua turned to his left. The Eye of Tekhenu in Ramanna poked over the horizon to their south.

He leaned forward, gripping Philaena's long white mane. The air rushed past at high speed. The stunning patchwork landscape stretching below under the light of the rising moon was breathtaking. It felt exhilarating. A strange distortion blanketed the entire sky above him as he battled to hold his head straight in the oncoming air. All the stars rippled in unison as if a thin layer of water stretched out in all directions above. It was a curious spectacle. Ahead of them, a white-tipped mountain range ran north to south.

Philaena continued to accelerate. She flew so fast, everyone struggled to keep their eyes open, deafened by the noise of the wind. The winged horse soon closed the distance to the mountains.

After a few minutes of flight, Philaena stopped flapping and went into a gentle glide. The patchwork of fields below them gave way to rolling foothills. Philaena pulled her wings in and dove at the ground, tracing wide circles, weaving between the valleys. She leaned forward, sending them into a steep nosedive. Joshua's heart pumped as the rocky terrain rushed towards them, but Philaena extended her wings further and raised her head. This broke the speed to a gentle glide.

She flapped fast as the ground came up to meet them. With a last rapid flutter, the Metamorph came in for a soft touchdown. They still moved forward at speed, but the gallop slowed to a canter and then to a trot. Philaena came to a stop, panting. She bent her front legs so they could dismount.

As soon as everyone was off, the majestic white horse nodded its head, then turned and galloped away. After gaining speed, it spread its wings and once again took to the air, soon disappearing out of the canyon.

The landscape was a jumble of rocky boulders and crags with little vegetation. They were below the snow line, but the night air was still frigid.

A fantastic view of the entire valley stretched below them for miles, accentuated by the moon rising in the distance. The outline of the mountains on the far side of the river was the only thing obscuring the spectacular display of shimmering stars against the night sky. The River of Edufu snaked through the landscape, illuminated by the pale light of the moon.

"Well that's just great," Galleon complained. "You'd have thought she'd have at least told us where to go next. I mean, look around you. Can you see this Oracle anywhere? I certainly can't."

"You heard what she said back at the temple," Joshua said. "It's dangerous for her to be out in the open for too long."

"And it's bloody freezing," Galleon continued, ignoring Joshua. "And my feet keep getting stuck in between these rocks. Ouch! Honestly!"

"Relax," Andrew dismissed his Imp friend's complaints. "Look on the bright side. At least we're not being chased by some huge monster trying to kill us."

"Oh, I see. I guess you'd rather die of exposure then?"

"I'm already half dead just listening to your incessant whining. Keep on a bit longer, and it'll finish me off altogether…hopefully."

Galleon and Andrew laughed.

The Goat paced back and forth in His dark place. Jets of steam shot from His nostrils with each breath. The veins in His temples pulsated from rage. By his feet were pools of blood from where the malicious creature had tormented and killed His victims.

The rattling of a serpent closed in on the Goat's position from a dark corner. Then a giant snake came into view. It was the same monster He had sent to massacre the citizens of Alexur in the hopes of killing Joshua. The beast slithered all around the Goat in the shadows, coiling its body back and forth, before coming to rest before Him.

It raised its head off the ground to reveal a deep red underbelly. Its eyes were missing. Blood oozed from their sockets, trickling down the beast's scaly neck.

The serpent thrust its long tongue out, whipping it up and down. It hissed several times at the Goat. The half-man, half-beast glared at it as if He could understand what it was trying to convey.

The Goat's eyes shifted around the room. He contemplated what the snake informed him.

"The king has made his first mistake," he said. "Finally, I can put an end to the Oracle once and for good. GO," he shouted at his minion. "You know what to do."

The creature slithered off into the distance again and was soon gone.

CHAPTER TWENTY-TWO
A flame extinguished

"Let's spread out. There must be a cave or something around here somewhere," Joshua suggested.

They climbed over large boulders, searching for anything to suggest where they might find the Oracle.

"It would be helpful if we could do this in the daylight, so I didn't keep falling between rocks," Galleon complained. "Ouch! Honestly!"

"Over here," Andrew shouted. He was standing on top of a large rock, looking down at the rest of them. Behind him was a narrow opening in the rock face. Above the entrance, a cluster of boulders looked as though they might tumble any moment.

Joshua climbed up for a closer look. "That must be it," he proclaimed. "Come on."

Joshua and Andrew helped Sarah and Galleon up onto the large boulder, and they all shuffled down the other side. In the shadow of the moon, it was hard to see where they were treading.

"We're not going to be able to see anything in there," Sarah announced.

"Well, what about that light?" Galleon pointed to Joshua.

There was a faint glow seeping from Joshua's keeper bag. Joshua opened it up and pulled out the Orb of Memory which was glimmering.

"Why is the orb glowing?" Andrew asked.

Joshua shook his head. He held the crystal towards the front of the cave. There was just enough glow to light the path ahead. "Come on, then. Let's go. Just mind you don't disturb any of those," he pointed to the array of boulders above the entrance. "We don't want them crashing down on us or blocking our way out."

Joshua led them through the crack in the rock face. They walked through vast open chambers connected to each other through openings near the ceiling. Smaller tunnels at ground level allowed the group to pass between the caverns, but it was a tight squeeze at times. The Orb of Memory provided just enough light for Joshua to see where he was treading. Between the open caverns, a narrow tunnel wove back and forth. Water dripped down the walls. There was a damp smell in the air that sent shivers down Joshua's spine. Goosebumps formed on his arms and the back of his neck from the chilly air.

Several minutes into their exploration of the cave, Joshua reached a junction.

"Which way do we go?" Galleon whispered.

Joshua concentrated. "Hold on. I have an idea."

He put the Orb of Memory into his keeper bag. Placing his hands over the top, he obscured all the light from it. A faint flicker came from the right-hand tunnel.

"It's this way," he said, walking towards the soft glow.

As he neared, the glimmer intensified. He turned a corner into a spacious cavern. There, in the centre, was a small blue flame no bigger than his fist. It levitated just above the ground, with no source of fuel. A dozen rounded stones surrounded it. The cavern above stretched upwards, higher than they could see.

"Is that the Oracle?" Galleon's whispers echoed around the chamber, fading away after a few seconds.

Joshua crept around the ring of stones, staring at the blue flame and taking in his surroundings. There were two more openings opposite to where they entered.

"I need to speak to the Oracle," Joshua stared at the blue flame, his voice reverberating until the silence took hold again.

The flame erupted high into the air, warming the cavern. Everyone stepped back, shielding their eyes. After a few seconds, it died down, but to a much bigger, orange flame. Everyone stared in anticipation. Nothing happened. Joshua opened his mouth to speak again, but then a booming voice echoed around the chamber.

"The pure of heart may command the flame, for he is worthy that the Oracle may assist…"

With each word, wisps of orange smoke flew up into the ceiling, trailing sparks behind them. Everyone took another step back.

"Well, that answers that question," Galleon snorted.

Joshua and Sarah caught each other's eye. Sarah mimed the words *go on*, nodding at him with raised eyebrows.

Joshua took a deep breath. "I…I need your help. Can you restore my memories?"

There was a long pause. Then, the Oracle spoke again. Its words boomed around the chamber. "That which was taken from you, I am powerless to restore."

Sparks flew into the ceiling again, trailing thin wisps of smoke with each of the Oracle's words.

Joshua sighed. He paused before trying again. "Can you help me get into the Temple of Alexur?"

Once again, there was a pause before the Oracle spoke. "The temple has been sealed for a thousand years. That which you ask is beyond my power."

Again, sparks flew out of the flame and high into the vaulted ceiling.

Once again Joshua sighed. He lowered his eyebrows and pursed his lips together.

"…but there is a way," the Oracle said.

Joshua's eyes lit up. As he stood there, poised to hear what the Oracle next had to say, there was a blinding flash. The orange flame surrounded Joshua. It wasn't moving, and he could feel no heat. He was levitating in the middle of the cave. Everyone stood around him, but they weren't moving either — they were all frozen in time.

The Oracle then spoke to him. Her voice came from within his mind. It sounded like a young girl — sweet and tender.

"You do not need my help, Joshua. The power you seek is already of this world. Those with the power to enter the temple are without voice."

Joshua pondered these cryptic words. He wanted to speak — to question the Oracle further — but he was unable. He didn't understand why.

"That which was taken from you may yet be recovered. But you must beware, Joshua. Our time is running out. The power behind the throne cannot be trusted."

The Oracle's words quickened, becoming more pressing. "I fear for my people of this world."

Desperation in the timid girl's tone increased. "My time in this world will soon be at an end, for he who commands the dark forces is at hand."

The Oracle sounded like she was crying—a desperate plea. "Hurry, Joshua, before it's too—"

The voice cut off. The Oracle's words jostled around in Joshua's mind. He struggled to fathom their meaning or desperation in her tone.

Then, there was a high-pitched scream of panic. It was the Oracle's. The young girl's anguish rang out as if someone was torturing her. The screaming echoed through Joshua's mind. Waves of dread engulfed him, sending his anxiety soaring. Joshua wanted to reach out and help, but he was powerless.

There was another blinding flash. Joshua landed on a cold, hard floor. Another scream echoed around him. This time, it was a different timbre—much more familiar. Confused, he scanned for the source of the screaming. It was Sarah.

Two hands grabbed Joshua's shoulders, dragging him across the ground. It was disorienting, and he struggled to understand where he was. As he tried to get his bearings, he saw it. A huge black snake with blood-stained empty eye sockets was sliding into the chamber from an opening on the far side. It shot two jets of steaming liquid at the small blue flame levitating in the centre of the cavern. Someone pulled Joshua backwards. As they dragged him away into the darkness, the Oracle was extinguished, plunging the cavern into total darkness.

Christopher D. Morgan

CHAPTER TWENTY-THREE
The Temple of Alexur

In the pitch black of the tunnel, Joshua somehow scrambled to his feet. He followed the sounds of footsteps ahead of him. Reaching into his keeper bag, the young Woodsman fumbled for the Orb of Memory to help light up the way. He found it and held it up. Ahead, Andrew was squeezing through a narrow section of the passage.

"Here," he shouted to Andrew. "Take this on so we can see where we're going."

Andrew took the glowing orb and passed it forward. As Andrew squeezed through, Joshua stopped to listen. The sound of something approaching from behind sent waves of anguish soaring through him. He turned and pushed himself through the narrow gap and sped as fast as he could along the rest of the passage.

Once outside, Sarah handed Joshua the Orb of Memory, and he stowed it back into his keeper bag. The echoes of the pursuing snake grew louder.

"Hurry!" Joshua screamed. "We need to seal this off."

"Here," Andrew pointed to the rocks balancing above the opening.

"Everyone out of the way!" Joshua screamed.

He climbed the rock face to one side of the entrance and shifted some smaller rocks. The rattling sound continued approaching. The beast might emerge any second. He dislodged a rock and —

CRASH!

Several large boulders came tumbling down in front of the tunnel, sending dust and debris flying everywhere. Joshua leapt backwards and dove to the ground, protecting the back of his head with his hands.

After the dust settled, a pile of rubble blocked the cave. The rattling sound was gone.

"Quickly," he shouted, lurching to his feet. "Let's get out of here."

Joshua and the others scrambled down the boulder-littered slopes until they reached a clearing with a few shrubs. Panting, they knelt down behind the thorny bushes and waited.

Joshua's composure returned. He took several deep breaths. "Is everyone all right?"

"I think we're okay," Sarah stood up to peer over the foliage. "Doesn't look like the snake got out."

"Joshua, what happened back there?" Galleon asked. "The Oracle said there was a way to get into the temple but the next thing I knew, that monster showed up and extinguished the flame."

Joshua paused for a moment. "No," he shook his head. "The Oracle spoke to me. Don't you remember?"

Sarah shook her head. "We didn't hear the Oracle say anything after that, Joshua."

Joshua squinted into nothingness, trying to remember the Oracle's words. "She did talk to me. I was...well, I was inside the fire."

Galleon, Andrew and Sarah looked at each other with puzzled expressions.

"We didn't see you go into the flame, mate," Andrew shook his head.

"But I did. I swear it happened. You were all...sort of...frozen. Nothing was moving. You, the Oracle, everything was frozen in time."

Andrew and Galleon narrowed their eyes at him.

"What did the Oracle say?" Sarah asked.

Joshua thought hard again. "She said...the power to enter the temple was...of this world. At least, I think that's what she said."

"Well, what the bloody hell does that mean?" Galleon asked.

"Shhh!" Sarah admonished him. "Go on, Joshua. What else did she say?"

"She said something about the power behind the throne and that it wasn't to be trusted."

"What, you mean the king?" Andrew asked. "I thought he was on our side. Hasn't he been trying to help us?"

Joshua shook his head. "I...I'm not sure. It was all...sort of...cryptic. I don't know what it means either."

"Was there anything else?" Galleon asked.

"Yeah," Joshua nodded. "Yeah, I think so. There was something about entering the temple. That's right, she said the one with the power to enter it is without voice...I think. It's all a bit hazy. After that, she was screaming about her time in this world coming to an end. She was panicking—desperate. Then someone was dragging me across the floor into the tunnel. The last thing I saw was the snake extinguishing the flame."

Everyone pondered in silence the magnitude of what had just happened.

"It's all my fault," Joshua murmured, shaking his head and looking at the ground. "So many people have died already, and now the Oracle is gone."

Sarah reached over to Joshua and wrapped her arms around him.

POP!

Right beside Andrew, the same Kimalla he had befriended appeared out of thin air. It bounced up and down on its four limbs, squealing. Its big eyes glistened in the moonlight.

Andrew smiled at the beast, patting its head. "I'm sorry, little fella. I don't have any fruit for you at the moment."

The Kimalla stretched out its two front limbs. One extended to Andrew and the other to Sarah, sitting by its other side.

"I told you," Andrew said. "I don't have anything at the moment."

The Kimalla again bounced up and down on all fours, making squealing sounds.

"I do wish those things could talk," Galleon grumbled.

Joshua jerked upright. The Kimalla jumped up and down. Again, the animal held out its limbs to them.

"Hold on a second," Joshua said, his eyes widening further. It was like a light had just switched on in his mind. "*Those with the power to enter the temple are without voice.* That's it! It's them. It's the Kimallas. I bet you anything they can get inside. Think about it. They can appear anywhere, so why not inside the temple?"

"Well, that's all good and well but how does that help us?" Galleon asked. "We're the ones that have to get in."

Joshua stared at the Kimalla, its limbs extended. "Look at it. I think it's trying to tell us something."

Sarah's eyes narrowed. "Joshua, take my hand. Hold Galleon's. Galleon, you hold Andrew's hand."

They did as Sarah told them.

"Now, Andrew, you and I will take the Kimalla's hands."

Andrew and Sarah held their hands out to the Kimalla, who wrapped its long fingers around them.

SNAP!

The bushes and everything else disappeared. Joshua landed on the floor of a room. A fraction of a second later the others, along with Andrew's Kimalla, fell beside him, still holding hands.

"Okay, what just bloody happened?" Galleon asked.

A square chamber with sandstone walls surrounded them. A plinth stood in its centre. Everyone stood and dusted themselves down.

Joshua's eyes lit up. Sitting on the column was another golden pyramid — just like those from the other temples. The stone edifice was the same square shape as the base of the pyramid. Together, the two formed an obelisk.

"Hey, have you noticed?" Andrew asked, scanning the chamber. "There are no doors or windows."

"Don't let go of that Kimalla, Andrew," Galleon said. "If that bloody thing vanishes, we'll be stuck here."

Andrew reached down to grab the Kimalla. It leapt up onto his shoulder and sat there.

There were two glass domes above the pyramid. The moon shone through, bathing the obelisk in a pale light.

"I think we're in the head of the snake," Sarah said, looking up. "You know, the one in Alexur? Those must be its eyes."

Joshua walked up to the obelisk and studied the golden pyramid. It glistened with the moonlight bouncing off all four triangular sides. At its apex was a concave recess.

"All right," Joshua reached into his keeper bag for the Orb of Memory. "Everyone, stand around the pyramid."

They encircled the obelisk, holding hands. Joshua took the crystal and placed it on the pyramid. The moon's light penetrated the glass ball, lighting it up with a blue halo. Brilliant shards of intense rays shone out in all directions. Everyone stared into the orb, taking a sharp intake of breath.

CHAPTER TWENTY-FOUR

Remembering Archipelago

Joshua opened his eyes. The bright halo around the orb was no longer there. The pale moonlight amplified by the two glass domes above their heads was the only source of light. Joshua reached out and took the Orb of Memory from the golden pyramid.

"I remember now," Galleon gasped. "We were travelling through a place called Archipelago."

"And avoiding Palm Crabs," Andrew added, nodding.

"The Orb of Sacrifice," Sarah held her hand to her mouth. "That's what Luana had when she died. She had the Orb of Sacrifice. It was her death that activated it."

"But why?" Joshua asked. "What did activating the orb do?"

Everyone concentrated hard, but nobody could offer any suggestions.

"That wasn't the only orb," Galleon said.

"He's right," Andrew said. "There was the Orb of Sunshine as well."

"And the Orb of Flight," Sarah beamed. "Oh! That's how we got here, Joshua. We used the Orb of Flight."

Joshua bit his nails as he recalled. He, too, could now remember what happened to them before they arrived here in the Valley of Edufu, but there were still gaps in his understanding.

"Joshua," Sarah narrowed her eyes, "do you suppose these orbs have anything to do with whatever it is the king wants from you?"

Joshua shook his head. "I don't know. Maybe? Maybe there's someone I met that told us something important, or maybe we saw something—some weakness the Goat has. It could be anything."

"So, what do we do now?" Galleon asked. "I mean, we're not really any closer to figuring it out—even with our memories mostly restored."

"We should consider how we're going to get out of this place first," Sarah suggested.

"I still have the Kimalla," Andrew said.

"That's all well and good, but how do we know where we're going to end up next?" Galleon threw his hands in the air.

"I dunno," Andrew shook his head. "Do we even know where we're supposed to go next?"

"Well," Joshua sighed. "The king wants us to find him in the capital city of Astowan. But we don't even know which direction that is from here."

"Yes, we do," Sarah said. "Don't you remember? Jafar said that Astowan was at the north end of the Valley of Edufu. He said there were five temples we had to visit. So far, we've been to Asteena, Ramanna and now Alexur. If the last one is in the capital of Astowan, that means there's one more we still have to visit."

"But which one is that?" Galleon asked.

Everyone shook their heads.

Joshua yawned. "Well, wherever the next temple is, it'll have to wait until morning. I can barely keep my eyes open."

"We still need to get out of this chamber," Andrew reminded them.

Joshua nodded. "Well, then, I guess we'll have to hope your Kimalla knows what it's doing."

Andrew gestured for everyone to hold hands. Sarah reached up to the Kimalla sitting on Andrew's shoulder. The animal took Sarah's hand. Andrew was the last to close the circle, reaching up to let the furry beast take hold of his thumb.

SNAP!

King Ahmoses pushed the Eye of Horentus away from his face. He closed his eyes and lowered his head.

"What is it, my darling?" Queen Neferemu asked in a deep, slow voice. "Not more bad news, I hope? Always it is *bad* news with the Eye of Horentus."

The king kept his eyes closed and shook his head, a solemn look on his face. "A great flame has been extinguished from this world," he said in a deep, reflective tone.

A slight smile formed on the queen's face. She removed it when the king turned to her.

"This Goat is persistent. I will give him that," the king raised one finger in front of him, waving it back and forward several times.

"Did the Metamorph die?" the queen asked, tilting her head with her dark painted eyebrows raised. Anticipation was written on her face like she was expecting good news.

"No! She did not die, my love," the king placed the Eye of Horentus back into its corner and paced around the throne room. "She did exactly what her king asked of her. But at least the boy is still alive."

The queen's anticipation melted from her face, leaving disappointment in its place. She raised one hand and snapped her fingers. A valet hurried in bearing a platter with two gold-encrusted goblets and an ornate decanter of wine. He placed it on a table next to the throne. Another snap of the queen's fingers sent the servant scurrying back out of the room, grovelling all the way.

The queen turned to the tray and poured wine from the decanter into each cup. She then fixed a stare on the king. He was still pacing around the room. Without removing her eyes from him, she reached into her robe and pulled out a small glass vial, being careful not to let the king see what she was doing. A dark liquid swirled inside it. With one hand, she unstoppered the container and tipped its contents into a goblet.

The king continued pacing, making his way around to where the queen was standing beside the throne. She placed the empty vial back into her pocket and picked up the two goblets.

"Come, my darling," the queen said, a coy look on her face. "Let us drink a toast to the good fortune that the boy is still alive."

She held out the goblet into which she had just tipped the dark liquid. The king stopped pacing and turned to her. He stared queen Neferemu in the eye as he stepped towards her until they were face to face. He narrowed his eyes at the goblet in her outstretched hand. There was a pause. The king peered at the queen, fixing her with a long stare. Then, he smiled, took the drink and resumed his pacing.

The king raised the goblet to his mouth. Queen Neferemu's eyes widened, and she bit her lip. Her mouth opened, and she leaned forward, raising her eyebrows.

Then, the king threw his wine to the ground, shouting, "Enough of these games. Does the Goat not know with whom he is playing, hmm? Does he think His Divine Majesty will put up with his shenanigans? Hmm?"

The king stormed over to his throne, mumbling to himself. He raised his right hand and snapped his fingers. A servant hurried forward holding the king's writing desk.

"I must help the boy further. With any luck, he will soon be with me here in Astowan, and together we will put an end to this Goat once and for all."

Shaking his head in disgust, he took the peacock feather quill resting by the bowl of black ink and dipped the tip into it. He then wrote onto the blank piece of papyrus.

Christopher D. Morgan

CHAPTER TWENTY-FIVE
The Orb of Wind-2

Joshua landed on the floor in the cabin of Jafar's felucca, joined by the others an instant later. The Kimalla sprang from Andrew's shoulder over to a cupboard and rummaged through a box of River Palm fruits. It grabbed one before popping out of view.

"Is everyone here?" Joshua asked.

Sarah, Galleon and Andrew had confused expressions.

"Where are we?" Galleon asked.

"Back on the felucca, by the look of things," Andrew said, rubbing the side of his face. The Kimalla's toenails had dug into him when it leapt for the cupboard.

"I hope that giant snake isn't still here," Galleon said.

Joshua and Sarah climbed upstairs to investigate. It was dark outside with no activity visible anywhere. The moon hung over the city of Alexur. The head of the snake temple poked out above the cityscape. All looked peaceful. The stars were out in full force, glistening across the sky like a shimmering blanket of black velvet.

"Those must still be those fires from earlier," Sarah pointed to glimmers over the city.

Joshua heaved a big sigh. His shoulders sank. "I still don't understand it all, Sarah," he shook his head. "What is it I know that the king wants so badly? Even if I had all my memories back, I'd still have no idea what he wants of me. I only hope it's all worth it."

Sarah extended her arm around his waist. She pulled him close and rested her head against him. "Hopefully all our memories will come back to us in time," she whispered, heaving a big sigh. "I wonder when we'll get to go back home."

"Let's hope soon." He turned and gave Sarah a tender kiss on her forehead. She gazed into his eyes, wrapped both arms around him in a warm embrace, then kissed him. After their lingering hug, Joshua smiled. "Come on, let's go and get some rest. Something tells me it'll be a long day tomorrow."

The next morning Joshua awoke to find Sarah preparing bowls of fruit and nuts from a cupboard. Andrew and Galleon still snored. Dawn light poured in through the cracks in the upper deck. Joshua yawned, stretching his arms.

"How long have you been awake?" he wiped the sleep from his eyes.

"Not long. I've been going through the various fruits and things Jafar left us. There's quite a variety of foods here. You should try some of these." She handed Joshua a bowl of assorted fruits and nuts.

"Did someone say food?" Andrew yawned.

"Here," Sarah handed him a bowl. "Try to keep your food in your mouth or the bowl this time."

Ignoring Sarah's indignant look, Andrew nudged Galleon. He awoke with a start and also yawned. Everyone had something for breakfast. Even the Kimalla popped in briefly. It snatched a River Palm fruit from Andrew's hand just as he was about to bite into it and vanished.

"It's like he's tethered himself to you, Andrew," Galleon chuckled. "You make a lovely couple."

"Yeah, well," Andrew chuckled, taking a bite from a new River Palm, "jealousy will get you nowhere, my friend."

"So, what's the plan of attack today, Joshua?" Galleon asked.

Joshua didn't have a plan. He also wondered where to go next. "Well," he chewed on a piece of fruit, "I'm hoping the next temple is somewhere on the river between here and Astowan. The others have been on the river so it stands to reason the next one will be."

"The king is trying to help you get there, right?" Galleon asked.

"He seems to be."

"So, you'd think he'd make life easier for you somehow."

"Maybe Philaena will show up again," Andrew suggested.

Joshua bolted upright. "I wonder if…"

Everyone watched as he pulled out the rolled-up papyrus from his keeper bag. Sarah shifted the fruit bowls to one side. As Joshua unrolled the magical paper, his eyes lit up, and a smile spread across his face. Sure enough, there was a new message.

Hello Joshua. It saddens me to see a great flame of this world has been extinguished, but you are still alive, and for that, I am eternally grateful. I remain hopeful the rest of your memories will be restored before you arrive in Astowan and you will deliver to me that which you possess. For now, you must make your way to the Valley of the Dead just south of the great capital city of Astowan. There, Rashida will guide you further.

- Yours as always, His Divine Majesty, King Ahmoses III

Everyone stared at the message.

"The Valley of the Dead. That doesn't sound very inviting," Galleon fretted. "It still doesn't say whether that's on the river or not."

"Don't be so pessimistic, Galleon," Sarah frowned. "It can't be far from the river if it's just south of Astowan. At least we know that's on the river, right? I wonder who this Rashida is."

"Or what," Joshua said. "It might not even be a person."

"I wonder why it's called the Valley of the Dead," Andrew asked.

"I don't know. Let's not worry about that for now. We have to figure out how to get there first. Hopefully, this Rashida will find us when we arrive."

"What about the Kimalla?" Andrew suggested.

"But it isn't here," Galleon pointed out.

"We can use the Orb of Wind?" Sarah beamed with a sharp intake of breath.

Joshua pondered this idea, then reached into his keeper bag and pulled out the orb. He studied the carving of the lines that looped at the end on one side of the transparent crystal. He turned to Andrew, who raised his eyebrows and shrugged, saying, "It's worth a try. It worked the last time."

"Okay, let's do it," Joshua announced.

Everyone climbed the small set of steps through the narrow door to the upper deck. Andrew untied the lines to lower the mainsail into place and then steered the felucca out into the middle of the river. Sarah and Galleon helped Joshua to baton everything down.

"Hey, Galleon," Andrew shouted from the aft of the boat. "Just make sure you don't get too close to that barrel again."

"Hilarious, Andrew. Honestly!"

"Are we ready?" Joshua called out

Everyone nodded. They all tied themselves to something immovable.

With one arm wrapped around the main mast, Joshua held the Orb of Wind in front of him. With his heart pumping, he took in a deep breath, clenched his eyes closed, then blew hard at the orb.

Behind the felucca, the air darkened, as if a mini thunderstorm was forming. The turbulence intensified, generating an almighty gust of wind. It caught the mainsail, propelling the vessel at lightning speed up the river. Everyone grabbed on for dear life as the wind rushed past them like a tornado. Joshua struggled against the onslaught of the gust to open his eyelids a little. The terrifying gale screeched like a screaming mob. On either side of the craft, everything was a blur. He closed his eyes again as tight as he could.

The gust died down moments later. The turbulence behind them stopped, bringing the felucca to a halt. Once again, the front end dipped into the water, making an almighty splash. When the aft smashed down, it sent Andrew tumbling. Then the boat settled, water gushing over the deck, spilling down the sides and back into the river. After another couple of seconds, the mainsail stopped flapping. They had arrived.

Christopher D. Morgan

CHAPTER TWENTY-SIX
Valley of the Dead

Where they had arrived remained unclear. Joshua checked to see that everyone was still in one piece. Sarah untied herself from the forward bulkhead. Andrew picked himself up from the deck from where he had tumbled during the boat's rapid deceleration. Galleon was wringing out his tunic but otherwise no worse for wear.

Andrew's Kimalla burst into view, sending Galleon leaping backwards.

"Oh great," Galleon shouted, still dripping. He gave the Kimalla an indignant stare, his hands on his hips. "*Now* you bloody well show up? Honestly!"

The felucca continued forward but at a more modest speed, propelled by a gentle breeze. Ahead of them in the middle of the river, other vessels bobbed up and down with their sails raised. Moored along the riverbank were more boats. Rows of palm trees lined both banks.

"I can't see any buildings yet," Sarah stared into the distance. "Can you?"

Joshua shook his head. "Too many trees."

The felucca closed in on the other boats. People climbed up the palm trees, using machetes to hack away at bunches of fruit at the top. Others below held outstretched blankets to catch the falling clumps. Now and then a Kimalla would appear, attempting to snatch a handful of the fruits. Workers lunged at the animals each time but could never reach them before they disappeared.

People here were more effective at warding off Kimallas. Each tree being harvested had lookouts at its base.

Andrew steered the boat to an empty slot along the riverbank and tied it off. There were still no buildings visible through the palm orchard. Sarah noticed something odd through the hive of activity.

"Joshua, look!" She pointed to a girl standing still while everyone else walked back and forth. The child stared at them.

"Is she looking at us?" Galleon asked, tipping water from his boot.

"Could that be Rashida from the papyrus?" Andrew asked.

"Let's find out," Joshua led them off the boat and onto dry land.

All along the riverbank, small groups of workers were at the base of the trees, harvesting the River Palms. They twisted them from the stems and loaded them into crates. Others stacked the boxes two and three high onto their heads and walked them to the waiting vessels.

Andrew snatched a few of the fruits from a passing worker and slipped them into his pocket.

Joshua approached the young girl. A full-length white garment covered her entire body from her shoulders down to her bare feet. She was about ten years old. Despite her scruffy hair and dirty face, there was something about her. She kept staring at Joshua as they neared, and he saw that her eyes were different. One was a deep blue, but the other bright green.

Sarah bent down a little and gave the child a warm smile. "Hello. I'm Sarah. What's your name?"

The girl smiled back but said nothing.

"My name is Joshua. Are you Rashida?" Joshua smiled down at the girl, raising his eyebrow.

The girl shook her head, remaining silent.

Joshua's shoulders sank, and he sighed. "Do you know where we can find Rashida?"

She nodded, then turned and ran into the forest of palm trees.

"Hurry," Joshua urged. "Don't lose her."

They followed the little girl through the trees. She was agile, leaping over half-full boxes of fruits and dodging between people. She even swiped a ripe River Palm fruit from the top of a stack of crates as she wove through the workers going about their business.

After a few minutes of trying to keep the youngster in sight, they arrived at a tall stone wall made from the same yellow sandstone as every other structure in the Valley of Edufu. The edifice extended in both directions, marking the boundary of the River Palm orchard. The little girl ran through an open doorway.

Joshua and the others crept through after her. A curious spectacle awaited them on the other side. Dozens of small cubed structures sprawled before them. Each was about as tall as Joshua and several paces wide. Each of them had symbols carved into all sides—like those on the Eye of Tekhenu and Queen Raha's tomb back in Ramanna.

The tall wall they came through extended around the perimeter of the complex, forming a square enclosure. As the four of them wandered, there were dozens of these cubed blocks dotted about in a random formation.

"What do you suppose these are?" Joshua pondered aloud, running his hand along the side of one block.

"Tombs, I'd say," Sarah said. "Just like Queen Raha's tomb beneath the temple of Ramanna."

"So…do you suppose there are…d-dead p-people inside?" Andrew kept a distance from them.

"No," Galleon whispered, "they're alive."

"Alive?" Andrew gasped.

"Of course they're bloody dead, you idiot! Oh, come on, Andrew," Galleon chided. "You're not afraid of people who have been dead for thousands of years, are you?"

As they walked through the complex, there were many more much smaller stone blocks—perhaps hundreds—clustered around each larger one.

"I wonder if those are also tombs," Galleon pondered out loud. "Maybe slaves?"

"Not slaves," came an unfamiliar voice. "Warriors. They are the Army of the Undead."

CHAPTER TWENTY-SEVEN
Rashida

Joshua turned to see a woman standing there, smiling at him. She wore a white body-length garment similar to the little girl. One of her eyes was blue, the other green—just like the child. She had long blond hair tied into a ponytail that stretched to her waist.

"Did you say something about the, um...*undead*?" Andrew asked, a distinct tremor in his voice.

"They are the bodies of the warriors who protected the kings and queens. They do so still in the afterlife."

"So, these big blocks are—"

"Those are tombs of royalty from a bygone era. Welcome," she said, "to the Valley of the Dead."

The little girl came running between the stone blocks. She threw her arms around the woman, who smiled down at her.

Joshua's eyes widened. "Are you...Rashida?"

The woman smiled and nodded. "I am glad to finally meet you, Joshua. I've heard so much about you. King Ahmoses has been keeping me informed of your progress. I had hoped you would arrive soon."

Joshua's eyes lit up, and he could not prevent a beaming smile from forming. At last, he would get answers to all his questions.

"The king wants me to help him with his battle with the Goat. I have a memory he needs, but I don't know which."

The woman smiled warmly and took Joshua by his arm. "Walk with me."

Rashida led Joshua through the grounds. Sarah, Andrew and Galleon followed as they meandered between the tombs.

"Tell me, Joshua," she said in a calm and restful tone. "How much of your memory has already been restored? The king tells me you already visited the temples of Asteena, Ramanna and Alexur. Is this correct?"

"That's right. Each time we've used the Orb of Memory, I've remembered more about my past. Only...I don't know if other memories are still missing. Does that make sense?"

"It makes perfect sense. Memory loss caused by the barrier can be quite...disorienting. Since you are not from here, I can only imagine how difficult it must be for you. Strange, new places, people, sights and sounds..."

"And animals."

Rashida looked at him with a curious expression.

"Those Kimallas, for example. They just sort of appear and disappear...like magic. We don't have anything like that where we come from."

Rashida nodded with a chuckle. They carried on strolling.

"The problem is," Joshua continued, "I don't even know what the memory is that's supposed to be of help."

"The king has a magical artefact," Rashida said, her voice serene and gentle. "It is called the Eye of Horentus. Have you heard of it?"

"Philaena mentioned it—the king could *see things* with it?"

"The eye permits the king glimpses of other places. He knows you opened the Portallas before, Joshua. He has seen it. But he does not know how you did it. He hopes this is the memory you have. The king believes opening the Portallas in this world will weaken the Goat and peace may again be restored to this land. For many years the Goat has battled King Ahmoses."

"Philaena…" Joshua said.

"The Metamorph?"

"Yeah, well, she helped us to find the Oracle. She said something about the Goat's magic getting weaker?"

"That is correct. The king hopes that the Goat can be destroyed by opening the Portallas."

Joshua scratched his head, concentrating. "I *think* it might have something to do with these orbs but…I just…I don't know. Every time I'm close to knowing, it all just…slips away. It's so frustrating."

"I understand."

"The king sent me a message. He said I should come here and you would guide me further. Are you able to help me restore what's left of my lost memories?"

"I hope," Rashida winced. "There is a ritual written in the ancient scrolls I have been studying. It has not been performed for centuries."

"And this ritual," Joshua frowned. "This will restore the rest of my missing memory?"

"Perhaps. I hope. It requires the Orb of Memory."

"Oh, well, I have that." Joshua pulled the round crystal with the carving of a human head on one side from his keeper bag.

Rashida took the orb and held it up to her eyes. She twisted it, examining it from all angles, caressing it with her jaw open. A glint formed in her eye. "It is a wonder to behold," she murmured, gazing at the orb in awe. "I have always wanted to see the Orb of Memory. But Asteena is so far from here."

"Do you think the orbs have something to do with how to open the Portallas? I have the Orb of Wind as well."

Again, Joshua reached into his keeper bag, pulling out the Orb of Wind.

"This is what we've been using to get from temple to temple. We found it buried in the tomb of Queen Raha beneath the Temple of Ramanna."

Rashida's eyes widened further. She marvelled at the second orb with even more awestruck wonder. She held it close to her face. A tear formed in the corner of her eye. "Magnificent," she said in a slow, almost teary voice. "For millennia, it has been lost to time. And now…I hold it…in my own hands."

"Ahem," Andrew interrupted Rashida's moment of orb admiration. "Can we get back to that bit you said earlier about the, um…undead?" There was a distinct squeak in Andrew's tone.

Rashida lowered the orb and handed it back to Joshua. He replaced both crystals in his keeper bag.

Rashida turned to Andrew. "The people of the Valley of Edufu are superstitious. The only things you will find inside these tombs are the mummified remains of people long since dead. There is nothing you need to fear, my young friend."

"There you go! I told you so," Galleon nudged Andrew in the ribs.

"You said the king has been at war with the Goat for many years?" Sarah said.

Rashida nodded at her with a smile. Her expression then changed to one of concern. "Many of my people disappeared over the years. Some have even been tortured. It is the Goat that is responsible for the memory loss barrier—one of the ways he has tried to control the king and the people of this world."

"Yeah," Joshua nodded. "Jafar told us about that. He helped us when we were in Asteena."

Rashida let out a deep sigh and gazed at the ground, shaking her head. "Jafar has disappeared. I fear the worst for him. If the Goat has captured him…may his soul rest in peace."

Joshua's jaw dropped. "But, why would—" Joshua began.

"Because the Goat believes Jafar knows what you do. He is afraid the king will learn what that is."

"Why? I mean, why is the Goat at war with the king? The people here…they're all kind and peaceful. Surely, they're nobody's enemy?"

"Well," Rashida tilted her head with a resigned expression. "The Goat is fiercely jealous of anyone with magical powers. The king possesses the Eye of Horentus, and this is something the Goat won't tolerate. He will stop at nothing to defeat you, Joshua, or to prevent you from opening the Portallas."

She ceased her pacing and turned to the young Woodsman. "We have little time to waste, my friend. The sooner we restore your memories, the sooner you can help the king defeat the Goat. Only then will the people of this world be rid of the fear under which we all live."

Christopher D. Morgan

CHAPTER TWENTY-EIGHT
The Army of the Undead

The Goat stomped back and forth. He roared with rage, shaking His head violently. Off to one side, just visible in the dim light, bodies lay motionless in a pile, each contorted as though their bones were broken. Blood dripped from them. On the floor in front of Him sprawled another lifeless body.

"It will soon be too late!" He huffed, expelling jets of steam through His nostrils. He thrust one foot forward to strike the corpse, launching it into the air. It landed out of sight beyond the other pile of bodies.

"I *cannot* allow any further gateways opened. He must *not* leave the Valley of the Dead. If the king finds out how…the boy *must* die NOW!"

The Goat looked up into the dark recesses above him. He took in a deep breath and emitted an ear-splitting, echoing howl. Then there was silence. The Goat tipped His head forward. He peered into the darkness through His thick bushy eyebrows.

A faint scraping sound echoed in the distance. Footsteps were coming towards Him like someone was dragging something across the floor. Moments later, the source of the footsteps hobbled into the light. The figure of a body emerged —a mummy.

Dusty bandages encased it from head to toe. One of its feet hung at a sharp angle, dragging behind the limping monster.

The mummy stood before the Goat as if awaiting instructions. The Goat peered into the depths. More footsteps echoed from the dark. The Goat glared at the mummies coming into the light. Soon, there were dozens, dusty and falling apart like they had been decaying for hundreds of years.

"The boy must *not* escape the Valley of the Dead."

He held up His hand and swiped it curtly to one side. The corpses turned and hobbled back into the dark recesses of the Goat's lair. Soon, they were gone.

Rashida led Joshua and the others into a small building in the corner of the complex.

"What is this place?" Andrew asked. "There aren't any undead in here are there?"

Galleon nudged Andrew. "Will you stop blithering, man? Honestly!"

"This is where the ancient scrolls live," Rashida said.

Around them were recesses in the walls. Protruding from those were hundreds of rolls of papyrus. Rashida removed one. She blew away a thick layer of dust then unrolled the decaying scroll onto a stone slab in the middle of the room. She used pebbles to hold it down. Upon the page were similar markings to those on the other tombs.

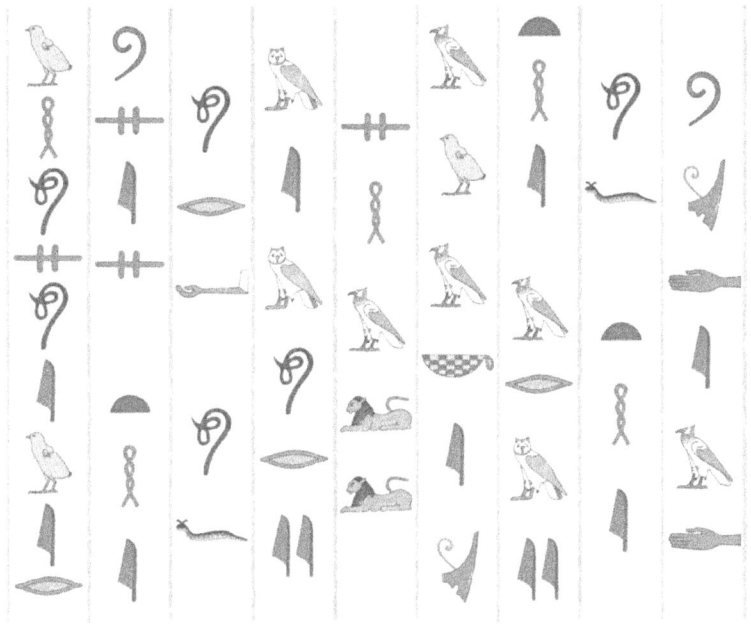

"Most of the scrolls here tell the history of the past kings and queens of the Valley of Edufu." Rashida leaned over with her face to the document, running her fingers over the writing.

"But not that one?" Sarah asked.

Rashida shook her head, continuing to read. "This one is a prophecy—a warning."

"A warning?" Andrew asked. "W-what does it s-say?"

Rashida smiled at Andrew. "My people are superstitious by nature. Many of the priests believe a handful of scrolls were written deliberately to scare people away." She turned back to the scroll and continued to run her fingers along the rows of symbols. "I doubt what's written here is of any real significance other than to ward off potential thieves."

"It w-worked. I-I'm already s-scared," Andrew bit his nails.

"Oh, for crying out loud, Andrew! What is the matter with you, you blithering idiot?" Galleon shook his head at his friend. "How can you be bloody scared if you don't even know what's written on it? I mean, it's not like you can read this strange writing, is it? For all you know, it could be the recipe for a River Palm Fruit salad or instructions on how to train your Kimalla. Stop being such a cry-baby."

"It's nothing to worry about," Rashida dismissed, turning the sheet of papyrus over and gesturing to markings on the other side. "This is what we're here for."

In the centre of the papyrus was a small cluster of unusual symbols with ornate flourishes around them.

"These look different to the other writing we've seen," Sarah leaned over the papyrus.

Rashida nodded. "This is the only scroll of its kind anywhere in the library."

"What is it?" Joshua asked.

"A spell," Rashida said

"A spell? What does it do?" Joshua asked.

"Well," Rashida said, with a slight wince. "If all goes well, I hope it will restore your remaining memories."

"Um," Andrew inched his hand into the air. "Did you say *if* all goes well?"

Rashida turned to him with a warm smile. "The Orb of Memory has never left the Temple of Asteena before, so this will be the first attempt. On its own, the spell is nothing more than a few words, but with the orb…" She murmured at the scroll, "I am hopeful."

"W-well w-what about that w-warning on the other side?" Andrew lifted the crumbling papyrus, ducking to see the writing on the underside.

"As I said," Rashida picked up the sheet and rolled it again. "It's superstitious nonsense. I'm sure the priests who wrote these words would enjoy seeing the fear that the mere mention of the prophecy has instilled into you."

"There you go?" Galleon chuckled. "For heaven's sake pull yourself together, man. Honestly!"

"If this works, Joshua. All of your remaining memories will return. And then…"

"And then I'll know how to defeat the Goat."

Rashida nodded. "Come, we should not delay." She took the scroll and led them out.

Christopher D. Morgan

CHAPTER TWENTY-NINE
The Awakening

Rashida led them out of the library, through the tombs and into the centre of the complex. There, in the middle of a large, circular, stone altar, was the unmistakable outline of a pyramid. It was like those from the other temples, with triangular sides shimmering in the midday sun. Atop it was a recess that fit the shape of the orbs.

"Please, if you would take your positions."

Joshua and the others spread themselves around the altar while Rashida unrolled the papyrus and weighed it down with a few pebbles.

Rashida gestured to the golden pyramid. "The Orb of Memory, if you please, Joshua."

The young Woodsman removed the crystal from his keeper bag and placed it on the pyramid.

Rashida raised her palms with her eyes closed and recited the spell. She repeated the incantation quietly at first, each time getting louder. Soon a wind picked up through the complex. As it intensified, it lifted dust and palm leaves, sending a cloud of debris flying. The air swirled around the altar, creating a visible column right above the pyramid. The Orb of Memory glowed with a blue halo engulfing it.

BOOM!

Joshua spun around. Behind him, cracks appeared in a small tomb. The fissures spread, breaking the structure apart as the turbulent air intensified. The ground beneath their feet rumbled as Rashida continued chanting with her eyes closed. Joshua struggled to see through the debris flying in the wind.

SMASH!

A smaller sarcophagus exploded. Joshua gasped, paralysed with fear as an arm clad in dusty bandages rose from the resulting rubble. Another two warrior tombs broke apart, and mummified corpses in each pushed themselves up out of the debris. Soon, dozens more slabs collapsed into heaps of crumbled rock with mummies crawling out of them. The decaying bodies staggered to their feet and limped towards Joshua and his friends. Fear coursed through his veins as they closed in from all directions.

The glow around the orb continued to grow. The column of wind above it widened further creating gusts so intense it was difficult to stand. Tombs of the Army of the Undead exploded everywhere. Dozens of mummies crept towards the altar, each with its arms stretched out in front of it. Some had limbs missing and were crawling or dragging themselves across the ground.

Rashida repeated the incantation over and over, her eyes still closed and her arms now raised high into the air.

Sarah screamed as a mummy reached them and grabbed onto her shoulder. Joshua pushed the mindless monster aside. It stumbled but scampered back to its feet again with its arms reaching forward. Hundreds of mummies closed in on the altar in the centre.

Two of the corpses clutched Rashida, dragging her screaming to the ground. More reached her and leaned over her.

The halo around the orb faded. Joshua dove into his keeper bag. He pulled out the Orb of Wind and blew at it as hard as he could. The turbulent column of air above the golden pyramid darkened. Then a torrent of wind rushed outwards from the altar, sending dozens of mummies flying out of the complex. Joshua and the others reached for each other and held on tight.

The deafening hurricane-force wind spread outwards from the altar, sweeping through the entire complex. Chunks of rock from the tombs tumbled in the air like leaves in the wind. Debris strewn with bits of mummies flew everywhere. The storm raged until every mummy blew away.

Joshua and Sarah remained clinging to each other as the screeching wind subsided. The column of dark air above the altar dissipated, and an eerie silence descended across the complex.

Joshua and Sarah opened their eyes, both reeling from the effects of the adrenaline coursing through their bodies. Joshua was still clutching the Orb of Wind in his hand. Andrew and Galleon were on the other side of the altar, but Rashida was gone. Joshua checked where the mummies dragged her to the ground. There was nothing there.

"Where did she go?" Sarah whispered, looking at where Rashida had stood.

Joshua reached for the Orb of Memory on the pyramid. It was no longer glowing. He took it and placed it back into his keeper bag along with the Orb of Wind.

"Is everyone all right?" Joshua asked.

Andrew rounded on Galleon with a frown. His small friend shuffled backwards with his hands held in front, palms facing forward.

Andrew folded his arms and squared off to the Imp. "'Stop blithering', he said. 'Nothing to bloody worry about', he said." Andrew contorted his face in anger, raising his voice and stepping towards Galleon. "Did you see those monsters? They weren't here to tell us how to make a bloody palm fruit salad!"

"I know what it is," Joshua blurted. "I know how to open the Portallas!"

CHAPTER THIRTY
Astowan and the Great Pyramid

Andrew ceased his admonishing and turned to Joshua.

"You do?" Sarah asked. "How?"

"It's the orbs," Joshua beamed. His eyes were gleaming. "We have to bring all three orbs together."

"Hold on," Galleon said. "Three orbs? But…there are only two of them."

Joshua froze, his jaw still open. Then his shoulders sank. He closed his mouth and narrowed his eyes as if the wind was knocked out of him. He paced around the altar, scratching his head. "No, no, no, there has to be another one…somewhere. Otherwise…"

"Maybe the king has one?" Sarah suggested.

Joshua stopped pacing and stared at her.

"Look, according to the king," she said, "we're close to the capital now. We should go there. He'll know what to do."

Just then, Andrew flinched as his Kimalla popped onto his shoulder.

Joshua's eyes widened. "Andrew! Don't let it go!"

ROARRRRR!

The Goat's rage was unrestrained. His screams echoed around His dark chamber, sending ripples through pools of blood on the surrounding floor. Dust fell from the dim recesses of the room.

"NO! This cannot be!" He screamed, pacing back and forth.

The hooves on His feet stomped, splashing through the blood pools. He stormed over to a pile of bodies and kicked one with such force the victim's head severed clean away. He thrust His hoof into the remaining heap of flesh, snapping the spine in two, leaving the body disfigured and twisted.

"So," the Goat said to himself, as he fought to regain composure. "If the boy wants to make it to Astowan, then he leaves me with no choice."

He raised his head and howled into the dark ceiling.

"Hurry! Everyone form a circle and hold hands. Let's hope it understands."

They did as Joshua asked. Andrew reached into his pocket and pulled out a squashed piece of River Palm fruit. The Kimalla jumped up and down on Andrew's shoulder, his eyes wide with anticipation.

"We need to get to Astowan," Joshua said to the animal. "We…we need to find King Ahmoses III."

Andrew's Kimalla stopped jumping and peered at Joshua, the pupils of its wide eyes contracted. The furry beast held its hands out. Sarah took one. Andrew completed the circle by taking the other.

POP!

Everything went dark.

Joshua landed at the base of a wide stone stairway with the sun beating down on him, followed by the others. Andrew appeared with the Kimalla on his shoulder and the piece of fruit still in his hand. The animal snatched the fruit and vanished.

Joshua spun around to get his bearings. Tall buildings surrounded them. Much more impressive than those from the other cities, these were bigger and intricately decorated. Many had gold fixtures and ornate window dressings.

People walked back and forth, paying no attention to the four of them standing at the base of the steps which stretched out on either side and climbed high into the sky, narrowing as they ascended.

"It's a pyramid!" Sarah exclaimed.

Joshua squinted at her with narrow eyes.

"Don't you see?" she pointed to where the steps tapered to a point high in the sky. "We're at the bottom of a pyramid."

Joshua held his hand to his face to shield his eyes from the sun. The pyramid was twice as tall as the one in Asteena.

"Look!" Andrew pointed towards a hole part way up the pyramid's side.

"Perhaps that's the entrance?" Galleon suggested. "If I were the king, I reckon this is the sort of place I'd be living, don't you?"

"Hey, there's another opening right up there near the top," Sarah squinted.

"Come on," Joshua urged. "Let's go."

They climbed the outer layer of the pyramid towards the lower gap in the centre. By the time they reached it, they were all puffing from exhaustion. Two leather-clad guards stood by the entrance, each with a tall spear held upright in his right hand. They were guarding an intricately carved wooden door made from two mirrored sections in the form of an arch. A large rectangular block of timber hung across it.

"HALT! WHO GOES THERE?" The soldiers thrust their spears forward, poised to attack.

"We're here to see the king," Joshua announced in a confident tone.

"What business do you have with His Divine Majesty?" one guard called out.

At that moment, a bell by the door rang twice. The guards lowered their weapons and stepped aside. The timber block in front of the doors rotated, allowing both to open inwards. Joshua and the others entered. The soldiers paid them no further attention.

Joshua's eyes adjusted to the low light inside the large chamber. Flaming torches hung on the walls.

"If you'll follow me, sir."

Joshua spun around to find a frail old man dressed in elegant robes standing there. The man was bent forward, leaning on a cane. He might have been over a hundred. He slowly turned and led them through a side passageway. After a few minutes of following, they arrived at the bottom of a narrow stairwell.

The valet gestured towards the steps. "His Divine Majesty will see you now."

Joshua peered into the dark passage and then climbed. Everyone followed him.

At the top of the stairs, another old man, wearing similar robes to the man downstairs, greeted them.

"This way, please, sir," he gestured with his hand.

Joshua led them into a long passageway with a high ceiling that stretched up into the pyramid. In front of him was a wall. Stone plinths lined against it every few paces, each supporting a magnificent, ornate vase designed with a shiny, blue surface. The art pieces were decorated with plumes of purple peacock feathers.

The king's servant walked them along the passage to where a large door, like the one at the entrance, was recessed into the stone wall. Much larger blue vases stood on the floor on either side of it.

The old man gestured for them to wait, and then he left.

Joshua's breathing increased. His anxiety was building. Sarah gave him a reassuring smile. Joshua turned to face the door. He reached out and knocked.

Christopher D. Morgan

CHAPTER THIRTY-ONE
An Audience with the King

With a metallic clunk, the huge double doors creaked backwards. Joshua led them into a large chamber with a high ceiling. A dozen muscular guards wearing leather strap armour stood to attention around the room. They stared forward through slits in their hoods. Each grasped a spear in his right hand.

On both sides of the chamber were a series of windows with stone plinths on either side of each, sporting magnificent vases and sculptures. Velvet curtains hung by the windows. The room oozed opulence.

Leading away from Joshua were a dozen wide steps, which he followed with his gaze. Like a flattened pyramid, they narrowed as they ascended to a plateau at the top. There, sitting on an ornate throne was a muscular man holding a wooden staff. Standing to one side of him with her hand on the man's shoulders, was a slender woman in a full-length purple gown. Her hair was tied up into a cone shape with golden ribbons. She wore stunning makeup with dark lines painted around her eyes.

The man raised his hand and, with a slight flick of his finger, beckoned Joshua to approach. Joshua turned to Sarah. She mimed *go on*, nodding with a smile. The nervous young Woodsman climbed the stone steps, approaching the king. His jaw still hung in awe of the opulent surroundings.

King Ahmoses III sat in comfort on his elegant throne. Intricate carvings covered the oversized chair with colourful peacock feathers woven in a lattice accentuating it on either side. His Divine Majesty leant back in his velvet-covered seat. The back rose to a point above his head, adorned with a crystal ball. It glimmered in the light streaming through windows that stretched high into the chamber. Atop the ball was a golden crown.

The king stroked his chin, tilting forward as if assessing Joshua. The queen caressed the king's shoulders. She eyed Joshua up and down, licking her lips.

"So," the king leaned forward. "For a long time, I have waited for this moment, young man." He tapped his finger on the velvet-clad armrest. "It is quite the journey you have been on, is it not? Hmm? But now you are here at last."

"You've been following my progress," Joshua said. He had been through a lot these past few days but through it all, the king had been helping him—sending him valuable messages and people to guide him. Although Joshua had never laid eyes on this man before this moment, strangely, he knew him.

"The Eye of Horentus has revealed some things to me, this is true." He gestured to the small mirror perched on the wooden staff in his hand. "But the eye cannot tell me what I most want to know. It cannot see into your head. Hmm?"

"You want to know how to open the Portallas."

The king leaned forward farther. His eyes gleamed with anticipation. "You have done this before," he nodded. "I have seen it with my own eyes."

Joshua nodded, thinking back to when he first opened the Portallas in Forestium and again more recently in Archipelago. He wasn't sure whether all his memories had returned, but he knew what he had to do—if only he had the third orb.

"You can do this again, yes? Hmm?"

Joshua took a deep breath. He heaved a big sigh and shook his head. As he said this, he couldn't help but notice a smile form on the queen's face.

Just then, there was a commotion. Muffled screams rang out from outside the chamber. There was a thud like someone falling to the floor. Then, everything fell silent. The guards exchanged nervous glances. The hair on the back of Joshua's neck stood up as he heard an unmistakable sound. It sent cold shivers down his spine.

"JOSHUA!" Sarah screamed.

Joshua spun around. Sarah pointed to a window. An enormous black snake was slithering through it. The soldiers on that side of the chamber ran towards it with their spears pointing at the beast. Before they knew what was happening, the serpent had lunged at them, sinking its huge fangs into their chests one after the other. Three guards fell to the floor as the monster continued into the throne room. The king's protectors rounded on it but the serpent raised its head and shot streams of steaming fluid in their direction.

The men screamed as the acid stripped through their leather armour, dissolving their skin. They collapsed to their knees, screaming in agony. The dark beast lunged at them each in quick succession. One by one, they fell to the ground writhing in pain. Within seconds, every guard lay motionless on the floor, blood oozing from his chest.

"Hurry!" Joshua shouted to Sarah and the others. "Up here!"

Sarah, Andrew and Galleon each ran up the steps away from the snake. It shifted its way around the outside edge of the throne room, its huge body still coming through the window.

A terrifying familiar white noise sounded from one side of the room. Joshua froze with fear as Wadjets slithered in through the windows. Hundreds of them fell onto the marble floor.

The two-headed snakes raced up the steps. Joshua and the others closed in around the king and queen. The noise from the hissing was petrifying. The tail of the giant snake slid through the window and it, too, started up the steps towards them. It raised its head high into the air, revealing a dark red underbelly. It thrashed its tail, sending echoes through the chamber. Dozens of Wadjets made it to the dais, scurrying towards them.

The huge doors through which Joshua and the others had entered burst open. Dozens of mummies hobbled through, dragging their feet and stretching out their arms. They climbed the steps towards the throne.

Joshua reached into his keeper bag and pulled out the Orb of Wind. With Wadjets and corpses now at his feet and the huge snake poised to lunge at them, he blew hard on the orb.

The crystal pulsated as a vortex formed above the dais. The air spun around them with such intensity it yanked the Eye of Horentus out of the king's hand, sending it tumbling through the air. Wadjets flew through the cavernous space in every direction along with broken pieces of mummies.

"HOLD ON!" Joshua screamed at the top of his voice. He turned inward and reached his arms out. Sarah, Andrew and Galleon grabbed each other, encircling the king and queen on their throne. Everyone held on for dear life, struggling to keep a grip on each other's wrists.

Joshua clenched his eyes tight as the air wailed around him faster and faster. There was an almighty gush of wind that blew outwards from the throne down the steps in all directions. Vases and sculptures went flying, crashing into the walls, sending debris out the windows. The velvet curtains ripped from their fixtures.

Moments later, the torrent of air subsided. The screeching wind died down. Within seconds, the turbulence dissipated, leaving the throne room quiet again.

Joshua opened his eyes. The king was on his throne, shielding his face. His wife still clung to the chair's back. The Wadjets were all gone. There was no sign of the enormous snake or the mummies.

Rubble and broken vases littered the floor around the base of the steps. What was an opulent room full of ostentatious finery now resembled a wasteland strewn with debris.

Christopher D. Morgan

CHAPTER THIRTY-TWO
The Portallas

The king stood up. An imposing man, he towered over Joshua. He placed his arms on the young man's shoulders. "I owe you my life, my young friend."

Still climbing down from the ordeal, Joshua panted. He smiled up at the king.

"And now, you will help me open the Portallas. Together we will defeat our common enemy."

Joshua shook his head with a mournful expression. "I...I can't. I mean, I want to, but I don't have the third orb."

King Ahmoses frowned. "The...third orb?"

"The Portallas will only open when I bring three magical orbs together. That's how it works. That's what I did before. Here," he reached into his keeper bag and pulled out the Orb of Memory to add to the Orb of Wind still in his hand. He showed both to the king. "I have two of them but not the third."

"Joshua!" Sarah gasped. She pointed to the glass ball sitting at the top of the backrest of the throne. The gust had blown the golden crown from it, revealing markings similar to those on the orbs in Joshua's hand. Joshua gasped with amazement.

"Do you know what that is?" Joshua gestured to the crystal with wide eyes.

The king regarded the orb atop the throne. "It is but a symbol of the power of the king. For centuries it has been here in this room."

"Can I see it?"

King Ahmoses regarded Joshua. He leaned over and removed the crystal, handing it to the young Woodsman. Joshua traced the outline of a crown carved onto the orb with his fingers.

Joshua's eyes widened. He passed the orb back to the king who sat back down on his throne to study it. "What does this mean?"

"I think this might be...the third orb!" Joshua gasped.

As the king revered the crystal, a smile formed on his face. The queen's expression contorted into a frown. She reached behind the throne and pulled out a dagger.

"The power is MINE!" She shouted.

Everyone backed away as she raised the dagger above her head. Then, in a single thrust, she threw her arm down and sank the blade deep into the king's chest, cackling a hideous laugh. The king let out a gasp, his head falling to one side. As he did, the orb in his hand pulsated. A green glow emanated from it, developing into a halo that grew until it engulfed the king.

The queen gasped, letting go of the dagger and taking a step back. The green light danced around the king, creating ripples in the air. As it did, the knife in his chest faded from view. The wound where it had entered shrank until it disappeared altogether.

The king gasped a deep lungful of air, bolting upright in his throne. He held the orb out to Joshua. "The Portallas!"

Joshua took the orb and held it against the others. All of them pulsated in unison. Joshua placed them on the floor before the throne. A swirling vortex formed over them. Everyone stepped away as the Portallas opened. The King stood up and moved to one side.

"NOOOO!" Queen Neferemu screamed, her hands shooting to her mouth.

Through the disturbance above the orbs, the Goat came into view. He glared at Queen Neferemu, shouting, "You have FAILED ME!"

Queen Neferemu shook her head, crying. "No, please, wait…"

The Goat rounded on Joshua. Letting out an ear-splitting roar, he yelled, "And now YOU WILL DIE!"

He raised one arm. A spear formed out of thin air in his hand. The Goat pulled the spear back and launched it through the Portallas in Joshua's direction. Joshua gasped, raising his hands to his face. The King reached over and pushed Queen Neferemu into the spear's path just as it came through the Portallas. It shot straight through her heart. She shrieked at the top of her voice before fading from view.

The Goat screamed, shaking his head. He raised his hand again. Joshua took a step back, expecting another weapon to form in the Goat's hands. The Goat looked down at his arm. He concentrated as hard as he could, getting more frustrated. Still, no weapon appeared.

"What's the matter? Getting weaker, are you?" Joshua shouted at the half-beast.

The young man stood defiant before the Portallas. The sum of all his anger rose from the pit of his stomach. Memories of all the people his nemesis had killed flooded his mind. His father, Protello, Luana, Jafar. All their faces flashed before Joshua's eyes as clear as day. He wanted vengeance for them all.

"Your magical powers are weakening," he pointed at the creature through the vortex, "your reign is ending." His voice grew louder and more confident. "And know this. I won't rest until you are dead. I will open every Portallas until I've destroyed all of your power forever. And when I do," he panted, finding untapped courage. "I'm coming after you." Joshua's breathing quickened. His face contorted with rage. He screamed at the Goat, "If it takes me the rest of my life, I will hunt you down and kill you!"

With one last roar of unrestrained rage, the Goat shook his head violently before fading from view.

Joshua sank to his knees, lowering his arm. He reached down to pick up an orb. As he touched it, there was a blinding flash of light. Joshua found himself suspended in time, caught within the orange flame of the Oracle. Everything around him was still. The others were stood frozen around him. All he could hear was the beating of his heart.

The Oracle's voice spoke. The sweet timbre of a young girl's voice echoed in his mind. "My dear Joshua. My brave, brave man. Your courage and determination have rid the children of this world from the one that wields the power. Never again will they suffer at His hands thanks to you."

Joshua struggled to understand. The Oracle's voice was the last thing he expected. "But…you died. I was there…in the cave. The snake, it…"

"I can never die, my dear Joshua, for I am eternal. For as long as my flame burns in any world, I cannot die."

"The power behind the throne. You said it wasn't to be trusted. All along…she was trying to kill him. But…I don't understand. She stabbed him. H-how…"

"The Orb of Power has not been needed since centuries past. It will always protect the rightful seat of power in this world."

Joshua's thoughts dwelt on those the Goat had killed. A sadness rose from deep within. "Will it ever end? How many more people will suffer because of him?"

There was a pause before the Oracle spoke again. "My dear Joshua, your destiny has been a perilous one, and one that is not yet fulfilled. For this, I must ask your forgiveness. But know this, my dear Joshua. You are surrounded by those that love you. From this, you have more strength than you know."

Joshua slumped on his knees with sagging shoulders, his energy spent. He had been through hell and back, experiencing a lifetime of grief and turmoil in the relative blink of an eye. More than anything, he yearned for home and a return to normality.

"How can we get back to where we belong? How can we get through the memory barrier that surrounds this world?"

His question sounded more like a plea.

"My dearest Joshua, you already have the power to depart from this world and to rid the people here of a terrible burden. You have the Orb of Wind. Use it well."

The echoes of the sweet voice faded. Another blinding flash brought Joshua's senses back to the throne room, where Andrew and Galleon were helping him to his feet. The king stood before him.

King Ahmoses III rested his arms on Joshua's shoulders and smiled. He pulled Joshua to him, giving him a grateful hug. Sarah cast Joshua a smile over the king's shoulder.

"I believe the Oracle has spoken with you? Hmm?" The King asked, releasing Joshua.

Joshua nodded. "Your people are now free from the Goat's tyranny."

"And I am free too, it seems. Hmm? And to think this woman...my queen..." The king sighed. He felt his chest where the dagger had entered. Looking down at where the wound was moments ago, he shook his head in contemplation. "And all along, she was conspiring with that monster."

"Something tells me you won't have to worry about the Goat anymore."

"This is thanks to you, I think. Hmm?"

Joshua smiled. He pondered the Oracle's words about using the Orb of Wind to rid this world of the memory barrier. He reached down and picked up the orbs. "Can you get us to the top of this pyramid?"

The king smiled. "Come, it is this way."

His Divine Majesty walked them to the back of the chamber. A passageway led to a series of steps up to the tip of the pyramid. From this vantage, the entire city of Asteena stretched out in all directions. They were so high up, the people in the streets below looked like ants scurrying around. All the buildings appeared as small dots in the distance. Above him were slight ripples on the clouds. It was the same distortion he saw while on the back of Philaena on the way to the Oracle.

King Ahmoses followed Joshua's gaze up to the sky. "The memory barrier," he nodded. "For many years it has loomed over this world."

"You'd better take cover," Joshua warned. Sarah, Andrew and Galleon all joined Joshua in a circle, holding onto each other's wrists tightly.

King Ahmoses III waved and took his leave. He bowed and was soon out of sight.

Joshua raised the Orb of Wind. He glanced at the others before taking a deep breath.

"We'll all need to do this together," he said. "On the count of three. One…two…THREE!"

Everyone blew as hard as they could at the crystal. It burst into light and a dark cloud formed high in the sky. The disturbance intensified, generating a swirling vortex stronger than Joshua had seen before. A massive column of air circulated above the great pyramid. Then, a gush of wind rushed up the slopes of the structure, shooting outwards in all directions. Joshua gripped his friends, holding on for dear life. He closed his eyes and clenched all his muscles as much as he could. Then, everything went dark.

Christopher D. Morgan

CHAPTER THIRTY-THREE
Epilogue

Joshua opened his eyes, but everything was still dark. *Have I been sleeping? Was it all a dream?* He blinked twice. Still, he couldn't see. Convinced he wasn't dreaming, he tried peering around.

It was disorienting at first, but his senses came into focus. He was on the floor, lying on one side. Reaching out his hand, he felt around him. Loose straw covered the stone floor. Joshua pushed himself up into a seated position. The light of a flaming torch flickered in the distance.

Joshua rubbed his eyes, trying to figure out where he was. He was in a small, dark, dank space. One wall of the room was missing where bars stretched from the ceiling to the floor. He stood up, reaching out to feel them. They were spaced apart enough to squeeze an arm through. Joshua pulled on a bar but couldn't move it.

There were no doors or windows. On the other side of the bars, a passageway led off in both directions. There were more bars across from that. Something stirred beyond them. Joshua squinted, shifting his head left and right to see through the two sets of bars between them. He recognised the outline.

"Sarah?" he whispered. "Is that you?"

Sarah stood up, looking around in a state of confusion. She walked up to the bars and shook them. Like Joshua, she, too, was trapped.

"Joshua?" She whispered back, "where are we?"

"I don't know. Do you have any doors or windows on your side?"

Sarah walked around her cell, examining all three walls. She came back to the bars, shaking her head.

Just then, there was a clanking sound, like keys rattling. A door at one end of the passageway between them opened, bathing it in light. The outline of a fat man approached them. He took the flaming torch from the wall and waddled up to Joshua. The bright light revealed him to be a heavily bearded man with a large, wonky nose. A thick, furry coat hung over his shoulders. Joshua shielded his eyes from the torchlight.

The man reached for a large ring dangling from his belt with a bunch of thick, metal, keys hanging around it. He found one and used it to unlock Joshua's cell. Joshua stood back as the guard twisted the key in the lock. It made a loud clunk, and he pushed the heavy gate. It creaked open.

"Right, you miserable maggot. Come with me!"

"Where are we going?"

"You've been sentenced to hang!"

The saga continues…

If you want to find out what happens next with Joshua, check out the rest of the Portallas series with more instalments imminent:

Joshua and the Magical Forest
portallas book 1

Joshua and the Magical Islands
portallas book 2

Joshua and the Magical Temples
portallas book 3

Joshua and the Magical Kingdoms
portallas book 4

Christopher D. Morgan

Glossary

For full descriptions, visit portallas.com

Alexur
A temple city in the Valley of Edufu.

Andrew
Andrew was welcomed into the village of Morelle as an orphaned baby when he was just two years old. Both his parents were killed in an earlier skirmish during the tribal feuds that plagued the North and West back then.

Army of the Undead
A large collection of mummy remains. The Army of the Undead exist to protect the kings and queens buried in the Valley of the Dead in their afterlives.

Asteena
A temple city in the Valley of Edufu. The temple is a pyramid with a huge statue of the king standing in front of it. The Temple of Asteena is where the Orb of Memory resides.

Astowan

A temple city in the Valley of Edufu. Astowan is the capital city of Edufu and home to His Divine Majesty, King Ahmoses III and Queen Neferemu.

Eye of Horentus

A small mirror affixed to the top of a wooden staff. King Ahmoses III can use the Eye of Horentus to keep track of Joshua as he makes his way north through the Valley of Horentus. However, the eye only shows a constrained view.

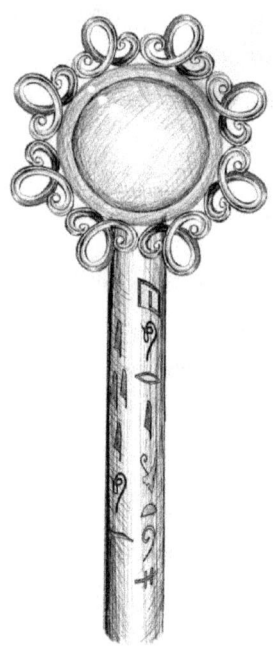

Eye of Tekhenu

A majestic obelisk located at the Temple of Ramanna.

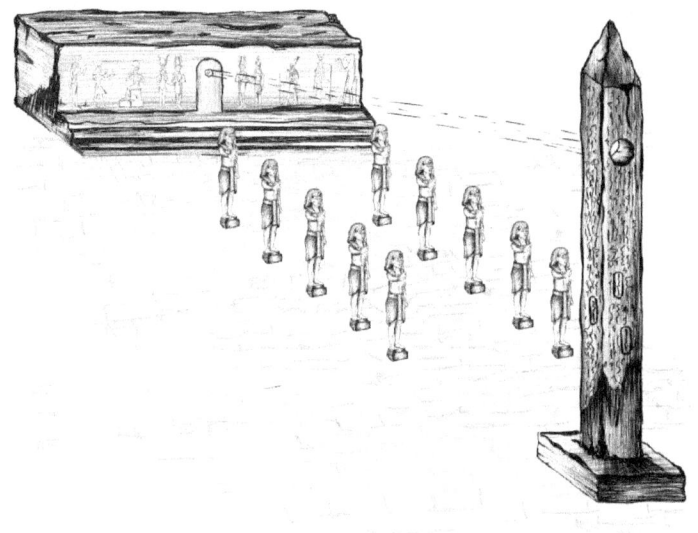

Felucca

A type of boat commonly found sailing up and down the length of the River of Edufu.

Goat

A mystical and reclusive magical being, the Goat is the embodiment of evil and malevolence. His origins are unclear. Half-man and half-goat, he spends much of his effort jealously guarding against anyone discovering the power behind various magical artefacts hidden throughout the worlds connected by the Portallas.

Imp

Imps are a diminutive race of people that have traditionally lived in the Southern Tip, a peninsula in the far south of Forestium.

Jafar

Assistant to King Ahmoses III. Jafar is sent to assist Joshua after arriving at Asteena in the far south of the Valley of Edufu.

Joshua

Joshua was born in Morelle in Forestium's far west. He is the firstborn child to Merinder and Sojath. Joshua grew up an only child but survives a sister who died during childbirth. Joshua's sister was not named and he was never made aware of her brief existence.

Kimalla

A small, furry monkey-like animal with large, green eyes. Kimallas can appear and disappear at will, typically preceded by a snapping sound.

King Ahmoses III
Current king and ruler of the Valley of Edufu. The king resides in the royal palace in the capital city of Astowan with Queen Neferemu.

Magical Papyrus
A magical piece of papyrus onto which the king can write messages which appear simultaneously on a similar piece of papyrus that Joshua possesses.

Metamorph

Metamorphs are an enigmatic race of beings with magical powers. They can change shape to become other people or creatures and they have healing powers.

Mirror of Prophecy

Magical mirror — may be used to see briefly into the future. Also provides a means for the Goat to see and reach into Forestium.

Oracle

An enigmatic being, the Oracle takes the form of a small blue flame that levitates. Hidden within the hollow of a rock exposed only at low tide, known locally as K'pia, the Oracle's location is unknown to the inhabitants of Archipelago.

Orb of Memory

Magical orb—restores lost memories.

Orb of Wind

Magical orb—can summon the power of the wind to drive boats great distances in a short space of time.

Orb of Power

Magical orb — provides a barrier to whomever is in power. The king cannot be killed if the Orb of Power is activated.

Powder of Heka

A magical powder which, when inhaled, can cause temporary memory loss and susceptibility to suggestion. The powder is highly illegal throughout the Valley of Edufu by decree of the king. It is obtained only via a black market — most commonly in the backstreets of Asteena. The powder is distilled from rainwater that has been infused with the magic from the memory loss barrier covering the Valley of Edufu.

Philaena

Philaena is the only known Metamorph living in the Valley of Edufu

Queen Neferemu

Wife of the current rule of the Valley of Edufu, king Ahmoses III

Ramanna

A temple city in the Valley of Edufu. Home to the Temple of Ramanna and the Eye of Tekhenu

Rashida

Rashida is high priest at the Valley of the Dead. She is an ally of King Ahmoses III.

River Palm fruits

Small, juicy fruit of the River Palm tree that is prevalent along the River of Edufu. Favoured by people and Kimallas alike.

River Slicer

Powerful and deadly animal that lives in the River of Edufu. River Slicers are known to drag people to their deaths.

Sarah

Sarah is the only child of Serelle and Albert, now the Elder of Jemarrah. Although they have no other children of their own, Serelle and Albert took in an orphaned girl, Isabelle, when Sarah was very young and raised the adopted family member as their own. Sarah and Isabelle consider each other sisters and are very close.

Scarab

Shady character that lives in the southernmost city of Asteena

Temple of Alexur

A temple in the form of a snake. This ancient structure sits half way between the capital of Astowan and the southern city of Asteena in the city of Alexur. The temple has no known entrance.

Temple of Asteena

A pyramid temple in the southernmost city of Asteena with a golden statue of King Ahmoses III standing guard. The Orb of Memory resides here.

Temple of Ramanna

A temple that resides in the southern city of Ramanna. Believed to be home of a long-lost magical power once commanded by Queen Raha.

Valley of the Dead

A temple city in the Valley of Edufu. The valley is home to a number of ancient tombs of kings and queens from bygone eras.

Wadjet

Deadly two-headed snake — one of the dark forces of the Goat's underworld.

Hieroglyph Alphabet

Use this alphabet to translate all the hieroglyphs found throughout this book

About the author

Christopher Morgan is a New York Times & USA Today bestselling author, blogger, IT Manager, graphics artist, businessman, volunteer and family man currently living in Melbourne, Australia. He spends much of his spare time volunteering for his local community. He creates visual learning resources for primary school children, which he markets through his company Bounce Learning Kids. He is also involved in local civics and sits on various community and council committees. When he isn't writing, Christopher visits schools to deliver presentations on writing and being an author.

Christopher was born in the UK and grew up in England's South East. At age twenty, he moved to The Netherlands, where he married Sandy, his wife of 30 years. Christopher quickly learned Dutch and the couple spent 8 years living in the far South of that country before they moved to Florida in 1996. After spending 7 years in Florida, Christopher and Sandy sold their home and spent the next 2 years backpacking around the world. Christopher has visited over 40 countries to date.

Whilst circumnavigating the globe, Christopher wrote extensively, churning out travel journals. He and Sandy settled back in the UK at the end of their world tour, where their two children were both born. In 2009, the family moved to Melbourne, Australia, where they now live.

Other books by Christopher D. Morgan

Novels

Joshua and the Magical Forest - Portallas book 1

Joshua and the Magical Islands - Portallas book 2

Joshua and the Magical Temples - Portallas book 3

Joshua and the Magical Kingdoms – Portallas book 4

Short stories

Sarah's Farewell - A Portallas Short Story

Galleon's Prime - A Portallas Short Story

Andrew's Mission - A Portallas Short Story

Anthologies

Ever in the After: A charity anthology in support of the 2017 Lift4Autism campaign.

Dawn of Hope: A charity anthology in support of the Cajun Navy and their relief efforts for those affected by hurricanes Irma and Harvey.